THE POWER OF THREE

TERI POLEN

Black Rose Writing | Texas

ISBN: 978-1-68513-501-0
LIBRARY OF CONGRESS CONTROL NUMBER: 2024942907
PUBLISHED BY BLACK ROSE WRITING
www.blackrosewriting.com

Printed in the United States of America
Suggested Retail Price (SRP) $19.95

The Power of Three is printed in Gentium Book Basic

*As a planet-friendly publisher, Black Rose Writing does its best to eliminate unnecessary waste to reduce paper usage and energy costs, while never compromising the reading experience. As a result, the final word count vs. page count may not meet common expectations.

For Janie, my niece,
former Lego apprentice,
and inspiration for Harper

THE POWER
OF THREE

PROLOGUE

Edinburgh, Scotland 1835

"Get the rope around her, Hans!" I yelled. My two brothers and I outnumbered the spirits we fought by one, but they presented a formidable challenge. After nearly a half hour, our combined strength began to wane. "Pull tighter!"

Hans struggled to bind the child ghost Iona with the blessed rope to hold her in place.

Karl and I worked together to restrain Iona's mother, Cora, an unnaturally strong spirit, as any mother fighting for her child would be. Iona, at the young age of ten, suffered an accident and died but hadn't crossed over as she should have. Instead, her anger over her too-short life consumed her and rooted her to this plane of existence. Cora now endured a similar fate. Distraught at her daughter's passing, she took her own life. Now the two of them were tethered to our world instead of moving on—mother defending daughter, daughter raging at the living.

Iona directed her wrath at her fellow school students. Her accidental death hadn't been their fault, but that didn't stop her from blaming them. In her quest for revenge, she'd lashed out and murdered five of her former classmates. Desperate for help, the school contacted my brothers and me. We'd earned a reputation for successfully handling cases of the paranormal nature.

Iona gnashed her teeth in rage and kicked at Hans, who barely dodged her attack. "Klaus, I need help! She's pulling away!"

We'd dealt with child ghosts before, but each life Iona took only increased her power.

"I've got Cora," Karl assured me, waving me away. "Go help Hans."

We'd trapped Cora in the middle of a salt circle, which prevented her from reaching Iona. If the circle was broken by so much as a grain, she'd escape. The cloud-filled sky above promised rain any minute, which would dissolve her makeshift cage. We needed it to hold off just a little longer.

While running to Karl, I pulled my iron rope from a hook on my belt. The combination of iron and Hans's blessed rope should weaken the spirit long enough for us to bind her. Sweat slicked Karl's face and blood trailed down his arms from wounds she'd inflicted.

Iona's otherworldly howls rivaled her mother's, and her face twisted with rage at our attempts to hold her. She had to be restrained before we could use our daggers to send her beyond the veil.

One of her arms escaped Hans's rope, and she twisted and fought to free the other. He tightened his grip and pivoted to the right to avoid her outstretched hand. Most—though not all—of the other child ghosts we'd encountered were confused and hadn't understood what happened to them. Once we'd explained the situation, they crossed over without further incident. Some were even grateful.

But Iona was far too furious. While Hans distracted her, I approached from behind then cinched my iron rope around her small body, pinning her free arm. She wheeled to face me, snarling and thrashing.

Cora fought desperately to get to Iona before we sent her on to the next world. She screeched and raked her ragged black fingernails toward Karl, who stayed outside the salt circle beyond the reach of her lethal claws. But his gaze remained fixed on the white salt. Even a gust of wind could break the circle. If that happened, Cora could escape and wreak havoc on us all.

Lightning flashed across the sky. Thunder boomed in the distance. The storm was nearly upon us.

"Karl, it's time!" I called.

He abandoned his guard over Cora and rushed over to us. We quickly pulled our iron daggers from sheaths on our belts. The hilt of each contained a gemstone that enhanced its power. Karl had a ruby for vitality, strength, and courage. Hans's contained a sapphire for loyalty, wisdom, clarity, and psychic ability. Mine held an amethyst for spirituality and transformation.

The three of us circled around Iona, daggers raised. Cora begged and pleaded with us to spare her daughter so they could remain together, but allowing Iona to stay in this world would only result in more murders of innocent children. She was a violent spirit now, not the sweet young girl she'd been before her death. We had no other choice.

I ignored Cora's pleas and nodded to my brothers, then we simultaneously plunged our blades into Iona. She screeched as her eyes rolled back in her head, and her small body trembled violently. Shock waves of dark energy ran up my arm, as if some sort of evil essence had forced its way into my dagger. I knew from my brothers' expressions they experienced something similar.

This had never happened before. Normally when we used our daggers on spirits, they disappeared with a flash of light or turned into wisps of smoke and floated away into the next dimension. None had ever resisted so tangibly. So forcefully. So painfully.

Cora's screams were pitched so high I was afraid they'd pierce my eardrums. I felt the need to cover my ears but couldn't let go of my blade. The shock waves were so powerful I had to drop my iron rope and grip the hilt with both hands. Hans and Karl copied my movements. We couldn't let go. Iona could escape if that happened, and we might never capture her again.

Static energy surrounded us, charging the air and raising our hair. Iona's body began to splinter into different pieces. Even the ropes couldn't hold her together. Pieces of her fell away, and Cora's shrieks echoed louder than the thunder in the distance. Heart pounding, I continued to grip my dagger and watched in horror as Iona gradually disintegrated until there was nothing left of her.

I'd never experienced anything so terrible. My brothers and I dropped our hands back to our sides and stared at each other, chests heaving in exertion.

Karl bent over and rested his hands on his knees as he peered up at me.

"What was that? It's never been like this before."

"I don't know." I shook my head. "Maybe the reverberation through the dagger was due to Iona's anger being so great. She hung onto this world with a tighter grip."

"Maybe," Hans said.

"Whatever it was, she's gone," I said. "She can't hurt another child. Or anyone else."

The three of us turned toward Cora. Dark hair hung in limp strands over her shoulders, and her eyes blazed with hatred for us. If glares were fatal, our lifeless bodies would be strewn about the grass.

Hans, Karl, and I readied ourselves to battle with Cora. We couldn't leave her in this plane. She might continue what Iona started. Children could still be in danger.

"You'll pay for what you did to my daughter," she spat. Every syllable dripped with venom. "You'll watch your children die as I watched my own. Death won't be quick or kind. It will be devastatingly painful. And when you finally shed this mortal coil, you'll be trapped here, never allowed to rest in peace. Your existence will be lonely as you helplessly watch your entire clan wiped from the face of this earth. Your lineage will suffer for generations beyond the three of you. I curse the Teller family and all its descendants!"

At that moment, lightning split the sky, thunder vibrated in my chest, and a downburst of wind swept around us. I watched, helpless, as the white line of the salt circle broke, its grains whipped into a vortex and hurled into oblivion. Hans, Karl, and I took a defensive stance and raised our daggers.

But Cora was gone.

CHAPTER ONE

"About time," Gid grumbled as we exited the highway to a two-lane road bordered by pine trees on either side. We passed a sign welcoming us to Mystic Harbor, North Carolina, population 64,783. Not exactly a booming metropolis, but large enough. The three high schools in the area shared a music teacher, a vacancy recently filled by our dad. Fortune had smiled so much on our family lately that I considered playing the lottery. I'd even welcome a small amount from scratch offs. Money was money.

Trees thinned along the road leading into town, and colorful houses on stilts took their place. I peered between the leggy beach houses, trying—but failing—to get a good glimpse of the ocean. When we came upon a busy boardwalk, the view opened. I stared, transfixed by the blue-green sea before me. Mystic Harbor was located on the Atlantic coast, something I was ecstatic about. The cause for this seemingly infinite road trip was due to Dad's recent good fortune. He'd inherited a distant cousin's house in North Carolina. Dad just wasn't sure exactly where said deceased cousin fit on the family tree. Macie wasn't a blood relation, but she was the widow of a distant Teller relative. Dad wasn't familiar with that side of the family, so they'd never been close. Apparently, that part of the tree had died off, and it had taken the estate attorneys a little over a year to locate any living descendants. Dad was the only Teller left. Besides us, I guess.

We'd never visited Mystic Harbor, but that wasn't an issue. What was important was the house. My family had never owned one. Our residential history consisted of rented houses when money was decent, and two-bedroom apartments when it wasn't. Basic necessities—food, clothing, and shelter—had never been a problem, but money had always been tight. My brothers and I worked part-time jobs from the second we were old enough. Money for phones, video games, and the car we shared came out of our own pockets. If college was in our future, it required our own savings, student loans, and scholarships. Both our parents worked—Mom was a former elementary school teacher and now tutored—but we weren't wealthy by any means. Teaching wasn't exactly a lucrative career. Mom also started working on her real estate license earlier this year for additional income. Finally owning a home free and clear along with the absence of rent payments would ease their financial burden and allow them to put more money toward other bills. And there were plenty waiting.

Music and art programs were often the first to be cut at schools, so we'd moved wherever Dad could find a job. Vacations were a luxury we'd never been able to afford, but one town where we'd lived was only a couple hours from the ocean, and we'd taken a day trip there. From the moment my feet hit the dunes, I felt like that was where I was meant to be. The smell of the salt air, the ebb and flow of the waves—I loved everything about it. Even the gritty sand in my shoes and clothes didn't bother me. I was home. And I hoped this place soon felt like home to me.

Vivid shades of orange and pink painted the sky as sunset approached. Quaint shops and a variety of restaurants lined the boardwalk, and people strolled its length while enjoying the summer evening. Pontoon boats, small yachts, and sailboats bobbed in their slips at a marina. Beyond that, the tip of a Ferris wheel on a pier peeked over the tops of sails.

I smiled widely, my knees bouncing in excitement. My feet itched to walk on the sand. I rolled down the window and inhaled the salt air. There was no better aroma in the world. Yeah. This was a place I could get used to.

"Maybe I can learn to surf after we get moved in," Lex said. He rolled down his window then hung out his head like he was the family dog. "How about it, Beck? You up for taking lessons with me?"

Gid snorted. I didn't take offense at his reaction because it was entirely warranted. On the scale of athletic ability, I fell somewhere between zero and negative one hundred. My broad-shouldered brothers inherited all the athletic ability and had played several sports between them at the schools we'd attended. I'd apparently waited in a different line when the sports genes were handed out. My lean frame was built for running. It was something I enjoyed and did several times per week. The solitude helped me clear my head, and I could also listen to audiobooks. Now I'd be able to run on the beach which was a thousand times better than neighborhoods or parks.

"Yeah, not happening." My gaze fell on a small corner bookstore with a help wanted sign in the window. Beside the sign sat a fluffy black cat who stared back at me as we passed. I mentally added it to the top of my list of places to check out once we were settled. My brothers had their sports, but I was drawn to books. The thought of being able to read on the beach anytime I wanted? That spelled paradise to me.

We passed through the bustling boardwalk area and drove a couple more miles out of town.

I looked at Google Maps on my phone. "It should be right around here."

Gid slowed the car as Lex and I searched for a mailbox or driveway.

"Is that it?" Lex asked.

What looked like the tip of a small red plastic flag peeked through a tangled flowering vine camouflaging the mailbox.

"Stop the car, Gid." He pulled over on the shoulder of the road, and I got out. Pushing the vines and dark flowering blooms aside, I uncovered the faded number 713 painted in white on the rusty iron receptacle. "Guess this is it."

After I returned to the car and closed the door, Gid pulled onto a narrow, gravel driveway. Overgrown shrubbery lined the sides, and I foresaw long, sweaty hours of yardwork in our future. Lots of hours.

"Guess Cousin Macie didn't waste her time on lofty aspirations like Yard of the Month," Lex said. "You know Dad's going to have us out here cleaning this up." he said, echoing my thoughts.

We pulled a small trailer containing the last few household items, but our parents had arrived the day before. They'd wanted to get a head start on moving in, but I thought it was excitement over the house more than anything. Since Gid was over eighteen we'd stayed an extra day to make sure nothing was left behind then turned in our house keys to the rental agency. Mom drove our other car—a ten-year-old minivan, used when we'd bought it—while Dad handled the large moving truck. Both were parked in front of a three-story, red brick Victorian house that stood tall and proud. I easily pictured Mom in a swing on the wraparound porch. With her love of gardening, pots overflowing with flowers would soon be added.

Intricately designed woodwork trimmed the numerous windows gracing three floors. A cylindrical turret at the right front corner of the house caught my eye, and I wondered if it was a bedroom. I'd have to beat my brothers to it if it was. The largest place we'd lived in was a three-bedroom rented house, and space to spread out was a foreign concept to us. This one was a castle in comparison, and the yard spanned acres. No moat that I saw. Maybe we could get a dog.

"Looks like I'll finally get my own room and not have to bunk with you losers anymore," Gid said. He pulled up beside our parents' van and stopped.

The three of us got out of the car and stretched while we gaped at the house. A real house. Not an apartment or a duplex. No shared walls with strangers. We'd even have a place to play video games while our parents watched TV in another room. No more using a weekly schedule Mom posted on the fridge. No more sharing a bedroom with my two brothers and listening to Gid's snoring and Lex's talking in his sleep. Mom could finally have the outdoor gardens she'd always wanted. Dad's dream of a separate office where he could actually hear himself think instead of listening to our chatter was within reach.

This house changed our lives.

The front door swung open, and little bare feet scampered across the porch. She ran down the porch stairs to the driveway, her chaotic auburn curls trailing in a wave behind her.

Our six-year-old sister Harper.

"You're here! You're here!" Unable to stop her momentum, Harper ran into Gid's legs.

He reached down, swooped her up into his arms, and kissed the side of her head. "Miss me?"

Her head bobbed, causing her to grimace as she rubbed her face against his scratchy beard scruff. Even if Gid shaved four times per day, he'd still have stubble. "Did you and Lex fight again?"

"Only because he took so many wrong turns." Lex smirked at Gid.

Harper held out her arms in my direction, and Gid passed her to me. Her hands wrapped around my neck as she hugged me tightly. Lex rummaged through his backpack then pulled out a small package. "Got your favorite gummy bears when we stopped for gas."

Harper squealed in delight and snatched the bag from his hand, then reached out and rubbed the side of his head. Lex had recently gotten both sides shaved, but not down to his scalp, and he'd left the top of his hair longer. He was a fan of temporary hair dyes and let Harper choose the colors. He'd probably sported every shade of the rainbow at one point. Right now, it was a cobalt blue. Even the shaved areas were softer than Gid's beard, and she seemed to like the way it felt. Maybe it reminded her of her stuffed animals.

Harper Teller had wrapped all three of her big brothers around her finger the moment she opened her smoky gray eyes. She was our family's miracle baby. It wasn't a planned pregnancy. Our parents had their hands full with the three of us, and with our financial situation more kids weren't on the agenda. But the thought of what my parents did to cause that pregnancy... nope, nope, nope. Not going there. Can't even think about it. That wasn't the miracle, though.

Harper saved our family. Before she came along, our parents seemed to bicker constantly over money. My brothers and I were too young to work and help out much. Gid was twelve and mowed lawns to earn some extra cash, but that small amount was only a drop in the bucket of our financial woes. As with most teaching positions, Dad's didn't pay well, but at least we'd had insurance. Mom still taught after Gid was born, but Lex and I came soon after. Paying for childcare was too expensive, so she'd started tutoring online. That meant a decrease in salary while there were more mouths to feed.

And then Mom discovered she was pregnant. It came as a surprise to all of us. Her pregnancy wasn't easy, and her doctor advised bedrest and stress avoidance. Like that was a simple thing to do. The arguments didn't stop completely but became more of a rarity instead of the norm. When we were told the baby was a girl, our parents were ecstatic. Girls were rainbows and tea parties, dance lessons and cute clothes. The three of us were smelly athletic shoes and dirty team uniforms, boy sweat and crappy t-shirts. The baby would be like a new start for our family.

Harper came early. Too early. We were unsure if she'd even live. We'd nearly lost her at one point when her heart stopped beating. The doctors revived her, but we were terrified. She remained at the hospital for weeks before she was healthy enough to be released. Mom stayed with her almost constantly, swearing she wouldn't leave until her daughter did. Dad worked and took care of us, but Gid, Lex, and I stepped up and did what we could.

The whole thing caused my brothers and me to mature quicker than other kids our ages, but we didn't mind. Our family had been on the brink of splitting up, and the three of us made a pact to do everything we could to keep that from happening.

Turned out, it wasn't our efforts that held us together. Harper needed all of us, and she saved our family.

Harper's mountain of medical bills only added to my parents' debt, and they were still paying them off. We didn't care. She was here, alive, and healthy. That's all that mattered. Once Harper came home, we all helped with feeding, bathing, and diaper changes—totally disgusting, but a labor of love. We even watched Harp while Mom took much needed naps. She said Harper was the best accident that ever happened to her.

I shifted my sister on my hip and studied the house again, still in disbelief we now owned it. Our parents stood on the porch, Dad's arm draped over Mom's shoulder. The front door of the house gaped open behind them.

"Ready to check out our new home?" Mom's eyes were bright with excitement. I remembered how she'd cried tears of joy when the attorneys finally tracked Dad down and delivered the news of his inheritance. We'd celebrated by going out for dinner that night to a restaurant that wasn't fast food. A rare experience for our family. Gid and Lex were so excited, they didn't argue all night.

"I'm the oldest, so I automatically get the biggest bedroom." Gid took the stairs two at a time up to the porch.

"The biggest bedroom is ours," Dad replied. "Harper has her bedroom, and the three of you can choose between five others. Plenty of space for everyone."

"Woohoo!" Lex brushed past me, leaped up the stairs, then dashed into the house behind Gid.

It would be cool if the turret was a bedroom, but I really didn't care which room I got. Just knowing I'd have privacy for the first time in my life was enough for me.

"Ready to show me your room, Harp?" I asked.

She nodded while shoving two red gummy bears into her mouth. Cherry, her favorite flavor. She wiggled out of my arms, then her sticky hand grabbed mine. She led me up the porch steps then through the double front doors into the house.

A blanket of icy coldness fell around my shoulders as I stepped over the threshold into the spacious foyer, and I shivered. Hairs on my arms stood straight up, and a feeling of wrongness twisted my gut. I wanted to grab Harper, get back into the car, and lock the doors.

"Come on, Beck." Harper pulled harder on my hand toward the spiral staircase leading upstairs.

What was this? Delighted smiles stretched ear to ear on my parents' faces, so they couldn't possibly feel what I did. The way Harper bounced around, it was clear she sensed nothing unusual. Gid and Lex mentioned nothing as they bounded up the stairs toward the bedrooms.

I refused to ruin this happy occasion for us. Maybe it was the unfamiliarity of the house that bothered me. It was a new place with strange surroundings, and something I'd have to get used to. Determined not to cast a damper on this moment for my family, I shrugged off the weird feeling then stumbled up the winding staircase behind Harper.

CHAPTER TWO

The first night in my own bedroom was a slice of heaven. None of Gid's geese honk snoring or Lex's incoherent babbling. No hitting my head on the bunk above me. I'd wondered if it would be too quiet or weird on my own. Maybe too quiet to even sleep after all those years of trying to drown out the nighttime noises. Instead, I'd opened the window to let in fresh air and even caught a hint of salt water in the breeze as I'd drifted off.

Not bothering to change from a t-shirt and pajama pants, I grabbed my glasses from the nightstand, opened my bedroom door, then headed left toward the stairs. My bare feet sank into the soft oriental rug as I padded down the hallway. Architecture and decorating terminology weren't in my wheelhouse of expertise, but even I could appreciate the features in this house. Wide corridors, a heavy wooden staircase with an ornately carved banister, stained glass windows, arched doorways. Leaps and bounds better than any other places we'd lived.

Dad had been thrilled to discover a piano in the living room. It was tuned and in excellent shape. He'd wanted to start Harper on piano lessons for quite a while. Gid, Lex, and I all learned, so it was her turn now. It came with the territory if you were the kids of a music teacher. My brothers weren't that crazy about playing, but I enjoyed it and still pounded out a song or two when I had the opportunity.

Mom loved Christmas, but other than a moderate-sized tree squeezed into a corner, decorations had always been sparse due to lack of space. Visions of what she could do with this broad staircase and its banister flitted through my head. Garland, white lights, red ribbons and plenty of family photos she insisted on every year taken in front of it. I could just imagine the smile on Mom's face and how happy she'd be. It was a beautiful home, and I was grateful the estate attorneys made the extra effort to track us down.

When I reached the bottom of the staircase, I noticed double doors off to the side that I'd missed yesterday. My stomach growled its disagreement, but hunger could wait a few more minutes while I peeked inside. Pushing open the double doors, I squinted into the morning sunlight streaming through floor to ceiling windows. Once my eyes adjusted, my mouth dropped open. It was a library, all the walls lined with shelves and every shelf filled with books. My heart thudded in excitement, and I grinned from ear to ear. That might have been an unusual reaction to some people, but not to a book lover. I saw hours upon hours of my future spent in this room browsing the titles and reading in one of the overstuffed leather chairs. If I spent a solid year in here, I wouldn't make a dent in the selections.

As much as I wanted to investigate, my stomach rumbled again, more insistent this time, and my mouth watered from the aroma of waffles and bacon drifting through the library doors. With a sigh of regret, I left. The room would be waiting when I was ready. We'd get acquainted very soon.

The sounds of my family echoed from the kitchen. Harper giggle-snorted at Lex's impersonation of her favorite cartoon character, and Gid asked if there was more milk in the fridge. The sound of the mower outside meant Dad had gotten an early start, and I was the last to stumble downstairs.

Although the architectural features of the house were beautiful, and all the furniture had remained, some areas still needed updates. The kitchen and bathrooms had been neglected for years. Not that I was complaining. The appliances worked and there were enough bathrooms that I didn't have to wait in line or pound on the door when Lex's love of extended showers ran into my scheduled time anymore. The faucet in the bathroom had sputtered and spat last night when I turned it on to brush my teeth, but after a minute the flow regulated. Who knew when it was last turned on?

"Morning." I raked a hand through my unruly auburn hair, nearly the same color as Harp's. It didn't matter what I did. No product or brush had ever tamed it. When I was younger, Mom usually gave up and shoved a baseball hat on my head. Gid and Lex inherited Mom's tamer lighter brown hair and coffee-colored eyes, but Harp and I got Dad's wavy hair and his stormy gray eyes.

I kissed Harper on top of her head, then checked the stove to see if my brothers had left me any food. You had to be quick in my family if you wanted sustenance.

Mom stepped out of the laundry room, a basket full of folded clothes balanced on her hip. "I put a plate in the microwave for you, Beck. Can you guys stay with Harper? I'm going upstairs to put clothes away and unpack boxes." She and Dad arrived two days ago, my brothers and I helped unload the truck completely yesterday. Everything was in the house now, but it would be days or weeks before it was unpacked and put in the proper place. The hallway and several rooms were a maze of boxes, but the quantity of our possessions seemed smaller somehow when moved into a house this large. Macie had left all the furniture, so at least we didn't have to purchase more to fill the rooms. Mom was already planning which items should be kept, which should be trashed, or—in the case of Macie's items—which should be sold to an antique store. Having too much stuff was a problem she'd never faced before. It was nice.

"Sure. Thanks, Mom." My plate was still warm, so I sat down beside Gid and reached for the maple syrup.

Gid hunched over his food like he was afraid a pack of wild dogs would burst through the doorway and wrestle it away from him. Mom repeatedly coached us on table manners, but they'd never taken with Gid. At least Lex breathed in between bites and used utensils. Well, most of the time, anyway.

Harp giggled as Lex pretended to steal a slice of bacon from her plate. He kept his attention on our sister while speaking to me. "Dad left a chore list on the fridge for us. Since you're up last, you get weed pulling. Gid's repairing porch stairs, and I'm trimming." We'd been responsible for yardwork and some minor maintenance at two of the houses we'd rented, so Dad made sure we'd learned the basic skills. When it came to repairs, Gid seemed to have a knack with a hammer. Considering his usual unsunny disposition, maybe giving him a hammer wasn't the best idea. Even Lex stayed out of his way when he wielded one.

"Gid's being growly today." Harper glanced in his direction.

I looked over Harper's head at Lex and raised my eyebrows in question. Lex held up three fingers. Which meant Gid was on his third cup of strong black coffee. We steered clear of him or kept conversation to a minimum until he'd downed at least three. Sometimes four. Getting between him and his morning brew never ended well or peacefully. Gid drank so much of it we'd debated if the amount of caffeine in his body was higher than blood.

I grinned at her as I squirted maple syrup over my waffles. "Growly is his default setting."

Her eyebrows drew together in confusion.

"He means Gid is always like that," Lex replied. "But he's growlier today than usual."

"What's up? You missed Beck and me last night? Your bedroom too lonely?" Lex waggled his eyebrows at that last line, and I threw a threatening glance at him. We didn't need to go there with Harper sitting right beside him.

Gid dropped his fork to his empty plate, then shoved his chair back from the table. "You guys slept last night?"

"Like the dead," I said through a mouthful of waffles, butter dribbling down my chin. Mom wouldn't be proud.

His eyes widened in disbelief, then he looked at Lex. "You're kidding, right?"

"Out the second my head hit the pillow."

"How did you two sleep with all those people talking?"

"What people?" I asked.

Gid rubbed his eyes in exhaustion, and dark crescents hung beneath them. "I figured it was the neighbors."

Lex barked out a laugh. "What neighbors? The closest one is half a mile down the street. Maybe you're just delusional. I've said it for years, you know."

"Or maybe he heard you talking in your sleep again. You jabber so much during the day you'd think your voice would want a break."

Lex glared at me.

"It wasn't Lex," Gid said. "After sharing a room for so long, I'd know that whiny tone anywhere."

"Television in Mom and Dad's room?" I asked.

Gid shook his head. "Not hooked up yet."

"Lex gaming? Cause it wasn't me."

"No gaming for me last night. Did the voices tell you to get out? You totally deserve to be haunted, Gid. How cool would it be to meet a ghost?" Lex might have been sixteen years old, but he routinely demonstrated the emotional IQ of a toddler. I'd been cursed by being born between my brothers. Unfortunately, that birth order also came with the title of mediator during their battles.

Gid flashed Lex a dark look then cleared his dishes from the table. "Well, whatever it was went on for hours. It sounded like a party downstairs, and I barely slept at all." After loading the dishwasher, he grabbed another cup of coffee, then went out the backdoor toward the garage. But not before he flipped off Lex. Good thing Harper couldn't see him, and Mom wasn't around.

"He probably dreamed the voices and slept more than he thought," I said.

Lex shoved the last of his bacon into his mouth. "Delusional. Maybe haunted, too. I called it."

"Gid's not lusional," Harper said, making me grin. She gently placed scraps of her bacon over her nearly untouched waffle to craft a smiley face. "Lots of people were here last night." Many imaginary friends of Harper's had lived with us over the years. Every move brought new ones. She'd even insisted Mom set extra places at the dinner table for a few of them. The way she invented detailed stories about these friends made me think Harper might be a writer someday.

"Great, so now Gid can hear Harper's 'friends'." Lex made air quotes on the last word.

I laughed. "And what are you doing today, Harp?"

She looked up at me and shrugged.

"Maybe you can pick flowers while I weed?"

Harper loved flowers, and I'd noticed several varieties in the overgrown garden. Keeping her outside with me would give Mom some uninterrupted time to unpack boxes.

"Yes!" she squealed enthusiastically as Lex covered his ears.

"Go get dressed, and I'll meet you outside."

"Since you're Harp wrangling this morning, I'll take care of your dishes." Lex shrugged when my jaw dropped. "Hey, I can be a semi-responsible adult at times. Just keep her away from me while I'm using the trimmer. We don't even know where the emergency room is yet, and I don't want to find out today."

* * *

It was a beautiful summer morning with temps in the mid-eighties. The humidity wasn't bad yet, and a warm breeze blew through my hair making it even more tousled. What could I say? It was a look.

Gid and Lex assumed I'd gotten the short end of the stick weeding the jungle of what was probably once an impressive flower garden, but I honestly didn't mind. Nonna, our grandmother on Dad's side, liked to garden, and before she died when we would visit her, I'd always enjoyed helping her. I liked digging in the dirt. It was peaceful, and I got a sense of satisfaction after planting flowers and vegetables. Like I'd improved the world just a little more. I'd also learned the difference early on between flowers and weeds. Lex and Gid would have haphazardly pulled up everything and left Mom with a flowerless patch of dirt.

Gardening wasn't quite as peaceful with Harper around. While I yanked weeds from the ground, she chattered under a shade tree with her favorite stuffed animals—Rex the purple tyrannosaurus— obviously—with bright red spots down his back, Loki the black cat with emerald green eyes—our love of Marvel might have influenced that one—and Percy the furry brown rabbit. She never ventured far without at least one of them and wouldn't sleep at night unless they were tucked under the covers with her. I needed to make a dent in the weeds before she'd be able to get to the flowers to pick them. Until then, she'd promised to play with her stuffies beneath the shade tree.

My mind wandered as I worked, making a mental checklist of things I needed to do. I planned to visit the bookstore we'd passed yesterday and ask about a part-time job. I hoped the owner would consider hiring students. My monthly phone bill was due, and I had enough to cover it, but I'd need to find employment soon. School registration began next month, and I wondered how this high school compared to the others we'd attended. This would be my third, and I was going into my senior year. Gid graduated last month before we moved, and Lex was starting his junior year. Hopefully, it would be the school we'd graduate from. Lex planned to check tryouts for sports teams. If the school didn't have a book club, I'd try to start one.

I suddenly noticed the chirping of the birds, which coincided with the absence of Harper's voice. I stood and looked over at the tree, lifting my hand to my eyes to shade them from the sun. Rex and Loki lay abandoned on the grass, but Harper and Percy were gone.

"Harper?" I walked around the tree to see if she was hiding. She'd slipped away from Mom in the grocery store one day to hide, thinking it would be funny. Mom was not amused. The manager locked down the store, and Mom was nearly frantic by the time they found Harper tucked in a corner behind the bakery counter. "Harp, you know what Mom said about hiding when we're not playing a game. Come out, please."

The sound of the trimmer cranking up flipped my stomach. Lex always put in his ear buds and listened to music when he worked outside, and if Harper sneaked up behind him, he'd never hear her. I bolted around the corner of the house and skidded to a stop, my heart pounding in my chest. Lex trimmed around the driveway, and Gid hammered away at the front porch. But no Harper in sight. Temporary relief washed over me. She wasn't in danger of getting hurt by yard equipment. Then my pulse ratcheted again. Harp was still missing.

But she couldn't have gotten far.

I hurried back to the garden to see if she'd gone back for her animals. Loki and Rex hadn't moved from their spots on the grass. As I scanned the large yard, an opening in the thick tree line drew my attention. If I'd noticed it, I'd be willing to bet Harper did, too. I sprinted toward it as I called her name. An overgrown dirt path led into the trees, and I panicked at the thought of Harper lost and alone in the unfamiliar woods.

As I dashed along the path, a sudden chill settled over my skin. Little sunlight penetrated the thick canopy of trees, so a cooler temperature wasn't surprising. But it seemed unnaturally cool, especially since I was sweating from all the running. Goosebumps rose on my arms, but I shrugged off the sensation and continued.

"Harper!" The path ahead seemed brighter, but I wasn't sure what lay beyond. What if there was a busy highway and Harper wandered into the road? That thought nearly paralyzed me. With no sounds of cars—or anything else—I figured the odds of a highway ahead were slim. Still, I picked up my speed.

Stumbling through the last of the trees, I came to an abrupt halt at the sight of a brick wall taller than me, the expanse broken only by grand wrought iron gates sporting matching bronze medallions with the letter T carved into them. Vines snaked up from the ground and wound through the iron spindles and across the top of the brick. The gate on the right was pushed open, leaving just enough room for a too-curious-for-her-own-good six-year-old girl to wiggle through. I should have known better than to trust her to stay put. Harp had an adventurous heart.

The gate screeched in protest as I pushed it open even further. Guess no one had oiled it for a while. It opened to a large cemetery that stretched for numerous rows. Patches of dense moss covered portions of the tombstones closest to me. I glanced at the names of the first two. Both listed Teller as the last name. With the letter T on the gates I'd just stepped through, I reasoned this must be the Teller family cemetery.

I lifted my gaze and surveyed the grounds. In the center of the sea of tombstones stood a towering, gnarled tree, its branches winding toward the sky. Standing underneath the tree was Harper, Percy clutched in her arms.

I sprinted in her direction, dodging the headstones and avoiding stepping on the graves. "Harper!"

She didn't look in my direction, but I heard her voice. She must have been talking to someone. Probably Percy since I didn't see anyone else around. If you asked Harp, she'd tell you Percy, Loki, and Rex spoke to her all the time.

She seemed surprised to see me when I finally reached her. I kneeled and pulled her tiny body in for a hug, squeezing her tightly even though she tried to wiggle free. "Harper, you scared me to death. You know you're not supposed to run off by yourself." Pulling back, I checked her over from head to toe. No scratches or blood that I could see. "Why did you sneak off?"

"Percy wanted to explore the trees," she replied, like it was a perfectly logical explanation. "So, we did. And then the lady in the blue dress led us to this graveyard."

"Lady in a blue dress?" My gaze darted around the cemetery, searching for the mysterious woman. Maybe someone had wandered onto the property. Being unfamiliar with the area, there could even be neighbors close by that I didn't know about. It surprised me that Harper was brave enough to come into the cemetery by herself.

Harper nodded. "She was here talking to me but left when you showed up. You scared her away."

Odds were the mysterious lady in blue was another one of Harper's imaginary friends. I'd probably learn more about her when we walked back to the house.

"If Mom hears about you wandering off, you'll be in trouble."

Eyes narrowed, she tilted her head to the side and pursed her lips. "Maybe you don't have to tell her?"

I knew what she was doing. At six years old, Harper was already a master manipulator with her three older brothers. We'd covered for her more than we should have, but she was so adorable the word no rarely passed our lips when it came to her. Lex took the rap when she'd broken Mom's favorite teacup. Gid claimed it was his fault the toilet overflowed. No one really believed him when Dad pulled out Harper's favorite Squishmallow. When Mom's birthday chocolates went missing, I took the blame. Was Harp spoiled? Absolutely. But she never pulled those stunts again.

So, even though I knew the right thing to do was tell Mom and Dad about Harper's adventure, I'd keep it between us. "Fine. But do it again, and all those secrets I'm keeping for you will gush out of me like a waterfall. Got it? No more running off."

A smile—made even more adorable because she was missing one front tooth—stretched across her face, and she wrapped her arms around my neck. "Thanks, Beck."

I stood and reached for her hand, afraid she'd take off again. She probably wouldn't, but I didn't want to take any chances. I studied the aged, dark tombstones in this section as we walked toward the gate, but most of the wording was illegible, worn down by more than a century of exposure and a coating of soft green moss. All the last names were Teller, that much I could make out. And there were so many. Family we'd never known. Generations of them.

I wanted to return and explore when chores weren't waiting. For now, I'd have to settle for quick glimpses of the names and dates as we passed by the headstones. My brow furrowed. Admittedly, I wasn't gifted in math, but even I could ballpark the ages at the time of death. Most of the deceased hadn't lived past their fifties. During the time of my great-grandparents and earlier, lifespans were shorter than today's, so maybe that was why there were so many young deaths here. There could be a medical history of cancer or terminal diseases in our family we didn't know about. That was kind of scary and seemed like important information we'd want to know.

This oddity piqued my curiosity, and I hoped to learn more from the books in the first-floor library I'd noticed off the kitchen. Maybe there would be a family history book that could help. These days, people interested in their genealogy could find more information on websites and even track down relatives. Depending on the cost, that might also be an option for me.

Harper swung our linked hands back and forth as we exited through the gate of the cemetery, Percy clutched to her chest with her other hand.

"What did you learn today, Harp?" I asked.

She puckered her lips and cut her gaze in my direction. "No running off without telling someone."

"Close. No running off at all. We don't know this area yet, and you can't venture into strange places by yourself. You should always have an adult with you. Got it?"

"But I had an adult with me."

I knew she was referring to the lady in the blue dress. "She was someone you didn't know. Everyone is a stranger to you unless you meet them with Mom and Dad or us, someone in your family."

"But she said she was part of our family. Her name was Anna Teller."

I blinked. Harper must have misunderstood her. The attorneys told my parents there were no other relatives around here, and that's why it had taken so long to track us down. She'd probably seen the name on one of the gravestones and used it for her imaginary friend. As I turned to close the wrought iron gate behind us, I glanced back once more to where I'd found Harper. Sunlight streamed through the canopy of trees overhead, but I'd swear a woman in a blue dress stood there watching us.

I wrote it off to my overactive imagination and dirty eyeglasses.

CHAPTER THREE

With Gid and Lex helping Dad paint the front porch, I figured it was a good time to take the car and head to the bookstore I'd seen on the way into town. I hoped the Help Wanted sign was still in the window. If I got the job, I also hoped the owner would work with my hours once school started. Books were my biggest obsession and being around them all day hardly felt like work to me. I'd been employed at a bookstore for several months at one of the other places we'd lived. It was the best job I'd ever had, and I'd hated to leave it. My biggest fear was getting fired for hiding in a corner reading. Which I'd tried not to do.

Hordes of people swarmed the boardwalk. With temperatures in the mid-eighties and the breeze coming off the ocean, patrons crowded outdoor patios and enjoyed the sun while eating lunch. Tourists strolled along the streets carrying bags from souvenir shops, saltwater taffy stores, and beach toy markets. A wide variety of colorful food trucks lined the sidewalk along the beachfront. I followed a sign directing me toward public parking at the next right turn.

I sidestepped people on the boardwalk as I made my way to the bookstore. Looked like this was the place to be on a nice afternoon. Was it this busy in the off season? Likely not. In most beach towns, the crowds died down after Labor Day.

After dodging a group of moms carrying shopping bags while wrangling kids with ice cream dripping from their hands and faces,

I finally reached The Book Haven. I immediately liked the name. Liked it even better that the Help Wanted sign still sat in the window.

A bell jingled over the door as I entered, and the hardwood floor creaked beneath me. With all the heavy wooden trim and the ornamental ceiling, the building was old but appeared to be well preserved. Creaking floors just added to the ambience. My gaze drifted around the store, taking in the tall bookcases and comfortable chairs stationed at various points. A children's section sat in the far-left corner, and a fake fireplace with small rocking chairs in front of it enticed young readers to spend time looking at books. Stuffed animals of fictional children's book characters sat atop shelves, and lights strung overhead made for an inviting reading corner. It was clear the owner put a lot of thought and time into decorating. Even if I didn't get the job, I'd have to bring Harper here. She loved books. Maybe not quite as much as I did, but reading made her top five favorite activities list.

Something rubbed against my leg. I looked down to see a fluffy black cat, the one I'd noticed in the window when we first arrived in town. It jumped up onto the shelf closest to me, sat on its haunches, and stared at me with its piercing golden eyes. Its gaze was intent, and I felt as if I was being weighed and measured. By a cat.

"Mr. Darcy is an excellent judge of character." A dark-skinned woman who looked to be a couple of decades older than my parents smiled warmly at me. Long braids adorned with colorful beads of orange, teal, and purple were gathered in a ponytail at the nape of her neck. Mr. Darcy leaned toward me, and I backed away a couple steps. "He wants you to move closer."

My experience with cats was limited. A girl I'd dated for about two minutes had one who'd hissed at me every time I'd gotten near him. He'd never attacked, but I'd kept my distance. "Um, he's not going to eat my face off or something, is he?"

"Of course not," she chuckled, seeming to enjoy my apprehension. "You can trust him."

I moved closer to the cat, unsure of what might happen next. He leaned forward, bonked his furry head against my own, then rubbed against my face. I turned toward the lady. "I don't speak cat, so can you translate?"

"You're approved," she laughed. "He doesn't head bonk just anyone. It's his way of showing affection. I'm Everline Jackson, avid reader and owner of this store. I know most of the locals, but I haven't seen you here before. Are you in Mystic Harbor on vacation?"

I pushed my glasses up my nose. "No, my family just moved here. I'm Beck Teller."

A brief expression of surprise flitted across her face. "So, someone's finally moved into the old Teller house? Feels like it's been empty for so long."

"Just a couple of days ago. My dad inherited it, but he didn't know this side of the family."

"I see." She nodded. "Well, what can I do for you, Beck Teller? Looking for some new young adult releases? Graphic novels maybe?"

I shoved my hands into my pockets. "I'm actually here about the part-time job. I have experience working in bookstores." Hopefully I didn't sound too desperate and eager. Because I absolutely was.

That warm smile slid across her face again. "Beck, I think this is a lucky day for both of us. If you want it, the job's yours. You won Mr. Darcy's approval, so you must be good people."

"Wow, thanks." It really was a lucky day. "Don't you want to ask me anything? Prior work experience? References?"

Everline tilted her head and narrowed her eyes at me. "I have a talent for getting a good read on people the first time I meet them, and I've learned to trust that instinct. Call it my superpower. I'm getting positive vibes from you, Beck. You said you had experience in a bookstore, and I believe you to be an honest person. Just don't prove me and Mr. Darcy wrong."

"No, Ms. Jackson. I won't."

"No formalities here. Please call me Everline. Now, when can you start?"

"Is tomorrow too soon?"

"Sure isn't. I've had this sign in the window for weeks, and not one applicant. Adults don't seem interested in part-time jobs, and teenagers want to spend their time on the beach or at other activities through the summer. The to-do list is overflowing, so come ready to work. I'll see you at 9:00 tomorrow morning."

"I'll be here. Thanks, Ms. Jac—um, Everline." I grinned from ear to ear in excitement at not only finding a job, but one that allowed me to be surrounded by books. Mr. Darcy closed his eyes in pleasure and purred loudly as I gave him a goodbye scratch under his chin, then I headed out the door and back to the car. The summer was off to a good start. Mystic Harbor was looking better every day.

• • •

Since the bookstore was only a couple miles from our house, I rode my bike to work the next morning. Lex left earlier to job hunt, and Gid volunteered to drive him. I didn't know what to do with that. The two of them rarely went places together, and for good reason. Last year they dropped by a Mexican restaurant after ball practice and were tossed out after an argument between them resulted in salsa and guacamole dumped over each other's heads. I didn't remember who wore which one, but I did know if they caused another public incident today, I wouldn't be dragged into it. I'd be at work and not responsible for their drama.

True to her word, Everline had plenty of tasks waiting. While I unpacked boxes full of new books, dusted shelves, and learned the register, Mr. Darcy kept watch over me. Our family never had a cat, but he was pretty good company. Honestly, I never knew cats had different facial expressions, but Mr. Darcy had no problem making his feelings known. When I accidentally knocked over his food bowl in Everline's office, his disapproving scowl said it all.

A steady flow of customers kept me busy through the morning, and I finally got a lunch break in the early afternoon. I'd packed a turkey and provolone sandwich and sat in the breakroom eating when Everline popped in to grab a soda from the small fridge. "So, is your family getting settled, Beck?"

I nodded, swallowing the last bite of my sandwich. "We are. The house needs some repairs and painting, but it's nothing we can't live with for now. My brothers and I help Dad, so we're able to divide and conquer. Makes it go faster, you know?"

Everline froze for a moment, then closed the door of the fridge and turned slowly to face me. "You have brothers?"

"Two brothers and a sister. Gid's a year older than me and Lex, a year younger. Then there's Harper, who's six."

Maybe I imagined it, but Everline paled slightly. "So, there are four of you? And your little sister is only six?"

I nodded. "Mom had her hands full when my brothers and I were younger, with us being so close in age. You'd think a later-in-life baby would have been hard on our parents, but my brothers and I help out, so in some ways I think Harper's easier for my parents than we were."

"Four siblings," she whispered, then closed her eyes and muttered something unintelligible. Something that strangely sounded like a prayer. But then her eyes opened, and a smile brightened her face once again. "Well, I hope things go smoothly with the repairs, and I look forward to meeting the other newest residents of Mystic Harbor."

Everline cracked opened her soda, then breezed past me as she went back into the store, leaving me to wonder exactly what had just happened. And why it raised the hairs on the back of my neck.

CHAPTER FOUR

"Where did you find the old clothes, Mom?" Lex asked, walking into the kitchen.

I needed to leave soon to get to work on time and was busy gulping down a quick breakfast of an everything bagel with cream cheese. Mom stood on a chair while she screwed in the hardware for blinds to be hung on the window over the sink. She'd worked in the kitchen for the past week scrubbing, mopping, and cleaning out the old fridge and pantry. Cleaners came in over a year ago after Macie passed away, but that much time with no humans present gave plenty of little critters the opportunity to move in. Dad set out humane traps for the mice, but it was left to Mom to clear away spider webs and droppings the mice left behind.

She looked down at her worn denim cut-offs and vintage concert t-shirt that had seen better days. "I won't make any best dressed lists, but they're not that bad."

"Not those. The ones you wore when you came into my room last night. The long dress and shawl."

Mom stepped down from the chair she'd been standing on, brushed off her shirt, and smirked at Lex. "Seriously? When's the last time you saw me in a dress? And I don't even have a shawl. That must have been some dream."

Lex grabbed a granola bar from the pantry and slumped down in the chair across from me at the kitchen table. "You spoke to me, but I couldn't hear you. Your lips were moving. But you picked up the drink I'd left on the nightstand in my room and put a coaster underneath it. I promised I wouldn't do it again."

"Now I know you were dreaming." She laughed. "I gave up on coasters with you boys years ago and tossed them out."

Lex's brows drew together in confusion as he bit off part of the granola bar.

Mom patted his shoulder on her way out of the room.

I wiped cream cheese from the corner of my mouth with my thumb. "And you said Gid was delusional. If it's genetic thing, glad it skipped me."

I wasn't sure what happened between them the day Lex was job hunting and Gid tagged along. Gid drove them to the boardwalk, but when he came home, Lex wasn't with him. Lex showed up completely drenched an hour later, having walked the two miles back to the house in the pouring rain. It was best to stay out of their drama unless it somehow directly involved or affected me.

Whatever the case, Joe's Beach Shack hired Lex, so something good came out of it. Gid also came home with a job at an oil change business, something he'd done where we used to live. He'd always liked working with his hands and had a knack for cars, just like he did with tools. College might not be in his future, but he'd promised our parents he'd look into community college classes once we got settled. While I'd have my nose stuck in a book and Lex watched action/adventure movies—the more explosions the better—Gid enjoyed bingeing home renovation shows.

Lex continued to chew silently. And two things were strange about that. One, he wasn't talking. Food in his mouth rarely prohibited that. Two, he'd let me get by with the delusional quip. He must really be bothered by what Mom said.

"What, so now you're dreaming about older women wearing shawls? Girls your age aren't mature enough?"

He raised his gaze in my direction, then went back to staring at the table as he ate.

"What's the deal, Lex?"

Thankfully, he swallowed before answering. "Someone was in my room, Beck, I swear. The lights were off, but with the full moon last night it was bright enough to see. I heard something rustling around. When I opened my eyes, I saw a woman gathering my clothes from the floor and then putting them in the hamper. After that she picked up my soda, wiped the wet ring with her sleeve, then pulled a coaster from her pocket and put it under the can."

"Like Mom said, you were just dreaming." I downed the rest of my orange juice.

He shook his head. "When I asked what she was doing, she said something, but I couldn't hear that, either. Then she sat at the foot of the bed and patted my leg like Mom used to do when we were little." Lex's eyes widened as he swallowed hard. "If it wasn't Mom, then who was it? And don't say I dreamed it because there's a coaster sitting on my nightstand to prove it."

That he hadn't joked about it by now spoke volumes. Either Lex really saw a woman in his room last night or he genuinely believed he did. Gid heard voices. Lex saw strangers. Maybe my sighting of the blue dress lady in the cemetery wasn't due to an overactive imagination or dirty glasses, after all.

What was going on in this house?

●　　●　　●

That evening, I sat on the wraparound porch reading. When Lex got home, I noted his grease-stained t-shirt and sweaty hair. Seemed his day was busy.

"Have you seen Gid?" he asked.

I narrowed my eyes in suspicion. "That's an odd question coming from you. What did you do?"

"I take offense to that implication." He feigned a look of shock. "I only have my brother's best interests at heart."

I snorted. "Now I know for sure you did something. Confess."

Lex sighed and flopped into the chair beside me. "Remember how I said I wanted to take surfing lessons, but they were too expensive?"

I nodded, still suspicious.

"Well, there's a guy I work with who's surfed for years and offered to give me lessons in exchange for something."

And there it was. "What was the something and how does it involve Gid?"

Lex rubbed the back of his neck and avoided meeting my gaze. "I might have promised to set him up on a date with Gid."

I snapped my book closed. "You pimped out our brother for surfing lessons?"

"What? No. Well... kind of yes."

I rolled my eyes. "He's going to kill you, you know."

Lex held up his hands in a stopping motion. "Wait, wait, wait. He's a nice guy, really. I think Gid would like him. Probably."

"Think I would like who?" Gid asked, coming from the direction of the garage. I swear it's like he sensed Lex's confession about getting him into something.

I tried to resist, honestly I did, but this was just too good. "Lex pimped you out on a date so he could take surfing lessons."

"You did what?" Gid's hands tightened into fists as he bounded up the porch steps.

Lex leaped out of his chair to face Gid. "Just listen, okay? He was working the front window the day you dropped me off for the interview, and he saw you. Today he asked me if you were seeing anyone." He shrugged. "And things just kind of evolved from there."

When Gid didn't immediately body slam Lex, I knew something was up. "There were two guys working the front counter. Which one?"

"The one with shaggy brown hair, about my height. His name is Aiden, and he'll be a senior this year."

Gid nodded but looked doubtful. "Is something wrong with him? Does he kick puppies or steal candy from kids?"

"What? No, of course not. He's a good guy. Just go grab a burger with him or something, no major life commitment. But when you discover he's your soul mate and want to express your undying gratitude, you can thank me by making me best man at your wedding instead of Beck. Or just give me cash. I wouldn't be offended."

By my calculations, the only reason Lex still stood seemed to be that Gid was attracted to Aiden. There were a few guys in Gid's past, but he'd had some bad breakups and first dates. Not that I'm laying blame anywhere, and Gid was far from the braiding-each-other's-hair-and-talking-about-our-problems type, but I got the impression a few of the breakups/bad first dates were because of his gruffness. It had gotten to the point that if Gid even gave a guy a chance, he waited for the ending before the relationship began. Noticing Aiden and not pounding Lex made me think Gid was ready to date again. But he needed a push. And Lex just gifted him one.

Gid dropped into the chair Lex had just vacated and swung a leg over the arm. "Sure. I'll go out with him. But if he's a jerk, I'll break your surfboard over your head."

"Duly noted." Lex looked relieved. "Well, I'm going upstairs to shower. All I can smell is fried seafood and burgers." He pulled a lock of his hair around to his nose and sniffed. "Even my hair smells like grease."

"This guy better be worth my time," Gid said.

Lex flipped him off before going inside, something they did to each other on a regular basis. Mom still only caught them half of the time. I figured it was their perverse way of expressing love for each other.

Just as the door closed behind Lex, an icy breeze whipped past me from the direction of the yard, like someone ran up the porch steps. No one was there, but the goosebumps on my arms said I hadn't imagined it. At the same time, Gid groaned and bent over, clutching his head.

"What is it?" I asked.

"Didn't you hear that scream?" he asked through clenched teeth.

"No." Then my heart took off at a gallop even though I'd heard nothing. "Wait, it wasn't Harper, was it?"

Gid sat back in the chair, eyes closed as he rubbed his temples. "It wasn't Harper. The scream didn't come from inside the house. It sounded muffled, or like it was in a tunnel. Same as the voices I keep hearing." Even after that first night, Gid still complained about hearing people talking. So far, he seemed to be the only one affected. "Between the voices and lack of sleep, I'm practically living on a diet of caffeine and ibuprofen."

Gid with his voices and Lex seeing people. Just last night Lex swore he saw me go into my room, but when he followed me inside to give me the order of fried clams I'd asked him to bring home from Joe's, I wasn't there. My room was empty.

"I'm going upstairs," Gid said. "At least I can block out the voices when I put on my headphones and listen to music. You coming in?"

"I think I'll stay and read for a while. It's nice out here."

"I've got the early shift tomorrow, so I can't drive you to work."

"No problem. I'll just bike there." Gid nodded, then went inside. Probably to take more ibuprofen. I got comfortable on the wicker couch cushions, then opened my book again, grateful for the silence other than the chatter of evening birds. That peaceful feeling didn't last long.

I'd only read a few pages when the chair across from me started rocking on its own in the still night air. I slammed my book closed, then hurried inside.

CHAPTER FIVE

I didn't have to be at The Book Haven until the afternoon, so the morning felt like the perfect opportunity to venture back to the Teller cemetery again. I'd only gotten a fleeting glance at the tombstones the day I'd found Harper there, but something was definitely weird about those death dates. So many of them were the same. Maybe in my panic to find Harp, I'd misread them. I hoped that was the case, but with all the unusual happenings in the house, I wanted to be sure.

The rocking chair on the porch last night disturbed me, and the image replayed through my mind as I laid in bed last night. We lived in a beach town a couple miles from the coast. Ocean breezes were a common event. Gid had just told me about hearing the voices in the house, so maybe he'd freaked me out more than I'd thought. I tried to rationalize what had happened. The porch was old with an uneven floor which could cause the chair to rock. Maybe I'd grown so used to breezes I hadn't felt it. Unlikely but possible. After Gid rose from the chair, it continued to rock because of the laws of physics. Also unlikely that it would rock that long and I'd missed it.

I'd decided to accept that the chair rocked on its own but not label it as a paranormal event. The odds were against it, so it was probably for some weird reason I'd never understand.

Purple morning glories creeped up from the ground and twined around the rusty wrought iron gates. They'd escaped my notice the first time I'd been here. Nonna's mailbox had once sported the same kind. She'd convinced me to help her plant them, and that day started my interest in gardening. I smiled at the memory.

The gate creaked mournfully as I pushed it open, and I was again overwhelmed at the rows and rows of graves. This cemetery seemed to be the final resting place for generations of Tellers. Cousin Macie's grave was probably here also. Even though my family would never meet her, visiting her grave seemed like the polite thing to do since we'd moved into her house. I wanted to thank her.

The darker, moss-covered stones on the orderly rows to the left I'd passed the other day looked to be the oldest, so I started there, planning to work my way to the newest and pay my respects to Macie on the way out. As I wandered over, the manicured grounds surprised me. Who'd been tending them since Macie's death? Would the responsibility fall to us now that we'd moved into the house? It was something I'd have to bring up with Dad. Even though we didn't know the deceased personally, they were still family, and it seemed disrespectful to let the cemetery become overgrown.

Kneeling before the first headstone in the row, I brushed dead leaves away from the dates on the bottom. *Klaus Friedrich Teller, loving husband and father, 1810-1870.* Only sixty years old. That seemed young to me, but things were different over a century ago, and people died younger. He shared the stone with his wife, *Anna Collins Teller, loving wife and mother, 1815-1872.* She'd lived longer, but not by much.

Anna Teller. Her name jolted something loose in my brain. Harper said that was the name of the lady in the blue dress she'd seen here. Though my sister had been nowhere near this grave when I'd found her, she must have passed it and read the name before I showed up. I grinned. She created new imaginary friends every place we moved.

I stood, pushed up my glasses, then studied the other rows of graves. How were all these people related? Finding a family tree book in the library sure would make this task easier. Thinking about that library got me excited all over again. I couldn't wait to explore it. Gid and Lex said they could always tell when I was thinking about books. Something about my eyes glazing over and a dazed look on my face. Whatever.

I strolled down more symmetrical rows and noted some of the names: Karl, Hans, Henry, Mary, Joseph, Edward, Thomas. So many names today were gender neutral, but not back in the mid-1800s or much of the 1900s. My full name was Beckett. Gid's was Gideon and Lex's was Alexander. Mom hadn't planned to shorten them, but when she was trying to wrangle three young boys, our full names were a mouthful. The abbreviated versions stuck.

Several of the deceased died at young ages, and not just those from over a century ago. Some were only in their twenties, and it made me wonder again about potential life-threatening conditions that could be inherited. A few had even been children. I wasn't a parent, but the thought of anything happening to Harper stole my breath, and I empathized with those children's parents.

The last row held the most recent headstones, and I paused to study them. Matthew, James, and Emily Teller. Matthew was the oldest, but he'd passed away at age twenty-five. James was born a couple of years later and died at age twenty-three. But they'd died on the same day. Their headstones listed each of them as son and brother, but no mention of Matthew or James being husbands. I wondered what happened. Car wreck maybe? Emily had only been ten years old when she'd died.

My gaze slid to the headstone beside them. Macie Williams Teller. It looked like Cousin Macie had been their mother. How sad that she'd outlived all three of her children. The pain she'd experienced must have been unfathomable, and she'd lost her sons on the same day. I imagined Mom losing two of us like that. It would destroy her. Dad, too. Sure, they'd still have two of us left, but a loss like that rips your soul apart, and it never quite fits back together the way it once did.

On the other side of Macie's grave was Thomas Teller, who I presumed was her husband. He'd passed away five years before their sons. My heart ached for Macie. She'd lost her husband and children far too early, then lived in this big house all alone until she died last year.

I turned and once again looked over the sea of graves before me. Dozens and dozens of them. Dad was an only child and beyond his parents, I'd never really known any other family on his side. But this branch of the Tellers wasn't a small family by any means. All these people were related to me in some way. According to Macie's attorney, my father was the last of the Tellers—other than me and my siblings.

What happened to this family?

•   •   •

When I got to the bookstore that afternoon, Mr. Darcy sat by the register, almost as if he'd been waiting for me. He gave me his usual head bonk in greeting. We'd never had a cat, but after just a few days with Mr. Darcy, I'd become a card-carrying member of the feline fan club. He followed me around, tail swishing, and I'd even started talking to him about the books I'd unpacked or shelved. In his cat language he replied in chirps, purrs, or meows. He was excellent company, although sometimes I suspected he followed me so closely because he liked jumping into the empty boxes to nap after I unpacked them.

Everline chatted with a customer in the mystery section, so I waited until they were finished to see where she wanted me to start today. After the customer left with three new releases, Everline turned to me and exhaled loudly. "It's been a busy morning. Lots of folks are buying books for the beach. I should have had you come in earlier."

"If something like that happens again, just call me." Extra hours meant extra money. "I explored the Teller cemetery this morning."

Everline was quiet a couple of beats, and her eyes tightened the tiniest bit. "I imagine it's pretty full."

I nodded. "My dad's an only child, and we only knew his parents. This side of the family was massive, but I never heard about these Tellers at all."

"Tellers have been in Mystic Harbor for more than a century. They were a sprawling family at some points, but their numbers dwindled throughout the years. They've certainly had more than their share of tragedies." She shook her head.

I leaned on the counter and pushed up my glasses. "Did you know my dad's cousin, Macie? The woman he inherited the house from?"

A wide smile brightened Everline's face. "I did. Macie was an avid reader and a regular customer. Such a lovely woman. She'd drop by, then we'd spend hours talking about books."

A fellow book lover. Sounds like I would have gotten along with Macie just fine. She'd probably filled several shelves in the library at our house. "I saw her grave this morning beside her husband's, along with three others. Were Matthew, James, and Emily her children?"

Everline nodded sympathetically. "They were. Emily died as a child, and Matthew and James were the last of the Teller line. Macie endured more pain than any person should ever experience. She was a strong woman, but I never understood how she survived it."

"Her sons died on the same day. Do you know what happened?"

Everline was silent for a moment as she pursed her lips. Almost as if she was choosing her words carefully. "Matthew and James were in the family business. They worked that day, and there was an accident. Both boys lived with her, and they were a close family. She was a shell of herself after that and rarely left the house after their deaths. I began delivering her book orders myself. We'd talk over coffee sometimes, but she was never the same. Macie was all alone, rattling around in that enormous house. It wasn't long before she quit ordering books. I'd still grab a few selections of my own I thought she'd enjoy and drop them off. But I insisted we sit on the porch. That house sent skitters down my spine." She shivered as if someone had dumped ice cubes down her back.

"How sad for Macie. What was the fam—" The bell interrupted me when it jingled as a group of customers entered the shop. She greeted them, then turned to me.

"We received a delivery this morning. Can you unpack those boxes?"

"Mr. Darcy and I are on it."

The cat jumped down and trotted to the stockroom, almost as if he'd understood what Everline said. Customers always came first, but Everline seemed relieved that we were interrupted. I had a weird feeling she hadn't been completely honest with me about Macie. Everline mentioned a family business, but I had no idea what line of work the Tellers had been in. And what had she meant about the house causing skitters down her spine?

Maybe I wasn't the only one who'd encountered rocking chairs that moved on their own.

•   •   •

Though customer traffic was heavy in the morning, it slowed in later afternoon, so Everline let me off work early. I walked across the busy street and down a block to Joe's Beach Shack. Every table was filled. Lex finished taking an order, then gestured with his head toward the beachfront deck so I headed in that direction.

The stars had aligned. Gid, Lex, and I finished our shifts within a half hour of each other today. Lex was wrapping up, and Gid was already at a table talking to Aiden. After their first date, they'd continued to hang out. I guessed Gid hadn't scared him off yet, which was a good thing. I liked Aiden, and I thought he could be good for my brother.

Lex had picked up surfing easily and said it was because of Aiden being such an excellent teacher. Just another reason to like the guy. And in contrast to the anger that was always churning just below

Gid's surface, Aiden was easy-going and calm. A go-with-the-flow kind of guy, and a balm when Gid got antsy over something.

Lex claimed Gid still owed him for fixing them up. Maybe we all owed him for that.

One morning last week I'd come downstairs to the kitchen for breakfast. Gid sat at the table hunched over a mug. If he was up, coffee was already made. I grabbed a cup from the cabinet above the coffee maker, then pulled the pot from the burner. It was empty. Rude. The power button was in the off position. I gently laid my hand against the side of the pot. It was cold. What was happening? Did I wake up in Bizarro world this morning? I spun toward Gid, ready to ask him what the deal was when I saw it.

A string with a white tag at the end draped over the side of Gid's mug. What the...was he drinking tea?

"Um, Gid? What's going on?"

He grunted in reply but kept his head down and played on his phone. His classic avoidance method.

I slowly walked over to the table, pulled out the chair, then sat across from him. With a potentially decaffeinated Gid in front of me, I knew not to make any sudden movements. The tag on the end of the string read Cozy Chamomile. "Do you need a quiet moment to yourself? Maybe some time to plan your day or ponder the meaning of life?"

He raised his head to meet my gaze, jaw tensed and eyes blazing. "Aiden said I should try tea, okay? It's supposed to promote relaxation and relieve stress and anxiety. You got a problem with that, Beck? If you do, let's have a discussion. If not, I don't want to hear another word about it."

Still in a state of shock, I could only nod quietly.

He stood, his chair loudly scraping across the floor. After picking up his cup of tea, he strode out the back door.

When Lex came downstairs ten minutes later, I was still sitting at the table in a daze, feeling like the world was slightly off kilter.

Yes, Aiden could be very good for Gid.

The restaurant deck was full of customers, and Gid and Aiden were so deep in conversation they didn't notice me or didn't care when I joined them at the table. Fine with me. I turned my gaze toward the rolling waves of the ocean while waiting for Lex. The tide was coming in. As long as we lived here, I didn't think I'd ever tire of watching it.

But then I saw something that eclipsed my interest in the incoming tide. Four girls around my age were gathered at the foot of the stairs leading to the beach. And I saw her. The rays of the setting sun touched her warm brown skin, and the wind gently lifted her long, curly chestnut hair away from her face. She tilted her head back, laughing at something one of her friends said. Her smile was radiant and would have chased away clouds on the rainiest day.

"Hello, Earth to Beck." Gid snapped his fingers in front of me, and I shoved his hand away from my face. He flashed a sly grin. "Someone catch your eye?"

"What? No. I was just... Shut up."

"That's a definite yes." Gid considered the group of girls and pointed to the object of my fixation. "It's her, isn't it? You've always had a thing for brunettes."

I grabbed his hand and yanked it back down to the table. If she turned this way and saw him pointing at her, I'd be mortified. The last thing I needed was to draw attention to myself. He'd already flustered me. "Yeah? Well, I could say the same thing about you." I gestured toward Aiden.

He ducked his head and smiled at my brother. Gid returned his smile and tucked a strand of hair behind Aiden's ear. Yep. He was a goner. The only other person I'd seen him do that with was Harper, and we were all putty in her hands. My brother was falling fast for Aiden. And to think he owed it all to Lex pimping him out in exchange for surfing lessons.

I looked back toward the steps where the girl was standing, but she and her friends had gone further down the beach. I felt... kind of sad. Since we moved so much, I hadn't put much effort into meeting anyone, let alone dating. Maybe it was time to change that. We were in Mystic Harbor permanently. No more packing or moving vans. I could actually have a real relationship and not have to worry about leaving again.

While I continued to stare at her, the girl glanced over her shoulder, gave a shy smile, then turned back to her friends. My heart stuttered. She'd smiled at me. Or, I think it was me. Really, it could have been anyone on this deck. I pretended it was me.

Lex dropped beside me and straddled the bench. "What's with the goofy smile on your face, Beck? You had that same look after your wisdom teeth were pulled and you were still under anesthesia when Mom brought you home."

"He found a girl," Gid replied.

Lex raised his brows. "Let me guess. Brunette?" Gid and Aiden nodded in unison. "Where is she?" He looked around the deck.

"About a hundred yards down the beach by now," Aiden added.

Lex half stood. "Should I chase after her and get her number? Because I know you won't."

"No!" I grabbed his forearm. "Just... don't."

Lex lowered himself back to the bench. "Beck, you know you have to actually meet a girl and talk to her if you want a girlfriend. Unless you're going with the fake girlfriend again like in... Where was it, Gid?"

"Memphis."

Lex pointed at me. "That's it. Memphis. What was her name again?"

"Sophie," Gid replied.

"Strange how we never met her, don't you think?"

"You know I can hear you. I'm sitting right here." They continued to ignore me. Stupid brothers. I wanted to punch both of them in their smug faces.

"Beck had a fake girlfriend?" Aiden asked.

And now they were dragging him into it.

Lex nodded. "Yep. It was a whole thing. Pretended she called him. Went out on fake dates. But none of us ever actually saw her. We'd always 'just missed her' or 'she was too busy to come over'." The air quotes made it infinitely worse.

I rolled my eyes. "She was real, okay? And what makes you think I'd ever want to bring a girl around the two of you?" Sophie and I had dated barely six weeks before we'd moved again. It's not that I didn't want her to come over and meet my family. Wasn't even that there hadn't been time, because there were opportunities. I was ashamed to admit it, but I was kind of embarrassed that my family lived in a two-bedroom apartment. It was just too small to cram one more person inside. We'd attended a large high school, and she knew who my brothers were from the sports they played. But they hung out with their friends at lunch, and Sophie and I ate together in a quiet place, usually the library, so we could read. She'd loved books as much as me and worked in the library as a student assistant.

Okay, and she'd also been a brunette. I have a type, and there's nothing wrong with that. But she wasn't imaginary.

I hoped I'd run into the girl on the beach again. I promised myself if I did, I'd talk to her.

CHAPTER SIX

"I never heard Grandpa talk about this side of the family." Dad and I were cleaning out the detached three-car garage while Gid and Lex trimmed the overgrown bushes along the driveway. I'd won the rock, paper, scissors round, so at least I was in the shade while the sun beat down on them. I only had spiders and their webs, years of dust, and the smell of gasoline to deal with. By the looks of the garage, it was pretty clear our deceased relatives hadn't been fans of spring cleaning. Half empty paint cans, tools that looked like they came from prehistoric times, wood scraps, and gas containers were scattered on the floor and shelves. It would easily take more than a couple of days to clean and organize. "Didn't he know about them?"

Dad pulled a bundle of crusty rags off a shelf, wrinkled his nose, then tossed them in the trash can standing between us. "I don't remember him ever mentioning much about this side. According to the information the attorney gave me, Macie was the widow of Thomas, whose grandfather, William, was a brother to my great grandfather, Joseph. Which made us cousins to the ninth degree as far as I could understand." Dad chuckled. "It's a complicated family tree. I remember my grandfather talking about a falling out with some family members, but it was a long time ago. I don't have any details, but I don't think one side associated with the other after that." He swatted at a large spider web in the shelf's corner. "From what the attorney said, the Teller family comprised multiple branches at one time, but now we're all that's left. There were relatives I never got to meet, and even more that you never met. It's kind of sad."

My mind drifted to the shelves of books in the library just waiting to be read and studied. I'd been so busy with work and chores that I hadn't been able to investigate. If I closed my eyes, I'd probably hear them calling to me. "Wonder what happened to wipe out so many family members? I was thinking there might be some family history books in the library. With all the old pictures of relatives hanging in the house, it seems like someone was interested in preserving our history and would have kept records. Maybe there are old diaries or journals."

Dad cast me a sideways glance and the corner of his mouth turned up. "Sounds like a project for you. I'm surprised you've held out this long, Beck."

Pushing my glasses up my nose, I nodded. "There's a lot to take care of with moving in and getting the house in shape. The books will wait." Though I said they'd wait, I was already mentally blocking out library time. The more I talked about it, the more I itched to get in there and explore every inch of the shelves. "Everline, my boss, knew Macie. She mentioned Macie's sons were involved in an accident at the family business that killed them. Do you know what kind of business it was?"

Dad climbed up the ladder to reach the top shelf and then handed down a box of old paintbrushes. "The attorneys said the Tellers had a successful furniture manufacturing business that went back for generations. There was a lot of machinery at their warehouse, and one son was pulled into it. His brother tried to save him, but neither survived. It was a freak—and grisly—accident. Macie had no interest in running the business after that, so she sold it after their deaths. Such a devastating thing to happen to her family."

"If she didn't take over the business, what did she live on after that?" Dead husband, dead children, living alone in this house.

Thinking about Macie also being penniless made me feel even worse for her.

Dad chuckled, which stirred up a dust cloud that made him sneeze. "She wasn't destitute, if that's what you're thinking. There was the money from the sale, and this house has been in the family for generations, so it was paid for years ago. The Tellers also lived within their means. Macie had enough to live on," he said, then paused. "I didn't tell you and your brothers, but besides the house, I also inherited some money."

"Are we rich now?" I knew we weren't, but couldn't resist asking.

"Don't quit your job." He chuckled. "I used the bulk of it to pay off some of our debt. It wasn't enough to cover all of it, so I also put a little in savings. Call it an emergency fund."

That was fantastic news. Lessening the mountain of debt that had loomed over them for so long took a huge amount of stress off my parents. I'm sure they slept better at night now. It also helped eliminate the biggest source of their squabbling from before Harper was born.

Dad climbed down from the ladder, then looked around the garage like he still couldn't believe all this was ours. "I appreciate all the work you and your brothers have done so far. It's a long to-do list, but we'll get there. Maybe even have most of it done before school starts in a couple of months." He pulled out his phone and checked the time. "I need to get going if I'm going to finish those errands before dinner. You got this?"

"Sure," I nodded. "I'll finish cleaning the last two shelves on this side and then help Gid and Lex."

"Maybe I'll take Harper with me to give your mom a break. She's emptying kitchen cabinets faster than Mom can stock them."

I grinned. When I'd come downstairs this morning, Harp was begging Mom to let her help, and Mom didn't have the heart to tell her no. Harper's way of helping was to drag everything out of a cabinet and inspect it or rearrange it, then move on to the next, leaving Mom to pick up behind her. Mom's level of patience had grown in direct proportion to the number of kids she'd brought into the world. She would have banned the three of us from the kitchen at that age and threatened us with a broom. My brothers and I had always spent a lot of time outside. Even the apartment complexes we'd lived in had grassy areas where Gid and Lex did their sporty things, and I always found a shady spot to read. It was her way of getting us out of her hair, I guess.

I tossed an old coffee can full of rusty nails into the trash, then moved on to the small blocks of wood. Why would anyone want to keep this? Did these people throw nothing away? They weren't hoarder level, but would the occasional weekend garage cleaning have been too much to ask?

One more shelf to go and then I could go swelter in the heat with Gid and Lex. And probably listen to them bicker over some inane topic. An old pile of dusty magazines joined the accumulating trash pile. When I turned back to the shelf to sort empty flowerpots, I accidentally rammed the back of my shoulder into the shelf frame. I winced in pain and rubbed it. That was sure to leave a bruise.

But then I noticed something odd. The side-by-side shelves no longer lined up properly. The one my shoulder hit was now sticking out a few inches on one side. My brow furrowed. There's no way my collision could have pulled it away from the wall like that. Dad had mentioned something before we started cleaning about them being anchored so they wouldn't topple over. I grabbed the side of the frame and gently pulled. With a loud creak, the shelf swung open a few feet to reveal blackness behind it.

I staggered backward and then tilted my head to the side in speculation. A door camouflaged as a shelf. What could be behind it? Stale air wafted from the opening. It was pretty clear the door hadn't been opened recently.

If trapped rats waited inside to escape, I'd be jumping on top of the ladder while they exited. Those furry bodies and weird tails freaked me out.

But all was quiet. Only silent darkness waited.

I grabbed a flashlight from another shelf and flicked it on. Sure, I could have used the flashlight app on my phone, but if I needed a weapon, the actual flashlight was heavier. Unsure if the batteries were still good, I sighed in relief when a strong circle of light appeared on the floor of the garage.

The shelf-door creaked as I opened it wider. I briefly thought about getting Gid or Lex before going in, but they'd have teased me for weeks if I did. It was just a hidden door, and it was time to see what was concealed behind it. Ideas swirled through my head as my imagination ran free. Dead bodies? A drug lab? A place to hide the crazy relatives?

Or people my relatives had kidnapped?

That wasn't outside the realm of possibility, since I knew nothing about them. They could have been serial kidnappers. Serial killers.

I rolled my eyes at myself and admitted my imagination cruised on overdrive. I blamed it on reading a lot.

The hidden room was probably nothing more than extra storage space for holiday decorations.

I shined the flashlight on either side of the door and discovered a light switch on the right. Would the electricity even work in here? Only one way to find out. I flicked the switch. Light flooded the room.

I frowned. What was this place?

The room was the same width as the three-car garage and extended back about twelve more feet. It surprised me we hadn't noticed the discrepancy in the measurements. We'd only been here a few weeks, so it would have been questioned eventually. Shelves lined the walls on one side of the room. They were full of containers of salt, numerous glass jugs filled with a clear liquid, ropes, and electronic gadgets I couldn't identify. One of them looked familiar but I failed to immediately place where I'd seen it. On the wall opposite the shelves was a pegboard holding more coiled ropes, rusted iron chains, and different types of guns. My parents wouldn't be happy about all these weapons on the property. I didn't know much about guns, but the sizes varied from the length of shotguns down to some small enough to fit inside a coat pocket. I browsed the shelves, picking up items and examining them, then moved on to the next shelf. What were these used for? Most were a mystery to me.

At the end of the room was a long, heavy wooden desk pockmarked with scratches and gouges that had seen better days. It might have been as old as the house. On top of it were stacks of files and books. No doubt the desk drawers and filing cabinets lining the wall to the right held more. So much paper. An old school computer that was cutting edge about twenty years ago sat atop the desk.

A variety of maps were pinned to the wall above the desk. One was a large map of the United States with pins stuck into nearly every state, their heads in varying colors. I'd seen similar designs showing states or countries people had visited or wanted to visit. I had a feeling that wasn't the case here. Others were maps of individual, well-known cities—Savannah, Georgia; Charleston, South Carolina; Boston, Massachusetts; New Orleans, Louisiana; and Salem, Massachusetts among them. The different colored pinheads must mean something.

Actual newspaper clippings were attached to the maps, some yellowed with age. Did print newspapers still exist? Words and phrases in the headlines jumped out at me—haunted house, spirits, graveyard occurrences, poltergeists, and unexplained happenings. Did our relatives have some kind of fascination with the mysterious and the macabre? Maybe they enjoyed keeping track of them, like a hobby. They could even have been ghost-hunter groupies, which was actually a thing.

I looked closer at the dates on the clippings. Some were over fifty years old. Others were as recent as ten years ago. When I lifted the edge of one to get a closer look at what it covered, it fell from the wall. Behind it was the map legend that indicated what the pin head colors represented—red for poltergeists, blue for specters, green for vengeful spirits, purple for violent spirits, and yellow for revenants.

Shivers rattled my spine as my mind struggled to fit the puzzle pieces together. All the strange instruments and guns on the shelves. Newspaper clippings that referred to supernatural entities. Pins in some of the most haunted cities in America. Color-coding corresponding to types of spirits.

Ghost hunter television shows weren't new to me. The "evidence" might be faked, but I'd watched plenty of them with my brothers and friends late at night when we tried to scare each other.

And that's when I remembered what the familiar gadget on the shelf was.

An EMF detector.

Spikes in electromagnetic field readings supposedly indicated the presence of ghosts. And there were loads of the detecting devices on these shelves.

I sat down hard in the desk chair, and it creaked beneath me. Everything I'd found in this room was related to the supernatural. Haunted cities, ghost hunting gadgets, files about spirits. The Teller family might have owned a successful furniture company, but now I wondered if they owned a side business people didn't know about.

Or maybe people did know.

I might be bonkers, but everything in this hidden room pointed to my ancestors being paranormal investigators. One question after another flitted through my head. I had a lot of investigations of my own to do. Apparently, it was in my blood.

•   •   •

"Don't fire me, Everline, I'm here." I struggled under the burden of books. I'd taken more than a dozen home to read. They weren't new releases, and as long as I returned them in the same condition I'd found them, Everline didn't mind. Thankfully, Gid drove today and dropped me off on his way to work, but we'd had to stop for gas—

honestly, we were on fumes and were lucky to make it to the station—and I was ten minutes late.

After setting the books on a table in the break room with plans to re-shelve them later, I hurried into the store to find Everline.

I stopped in my tracks. My breath whooshed from my lungs.

In the Young Adult book section was the girl I'd seen on the beach a couple nights ago. She stood in the stacks, reading the back cover of a paperback. Today her hair was pulled up in a high ponytail, and the morning sun streaming through the window highlighted shades of auburn mixed in with the chestnut.

"Beck, close your mouth before something flies into it," Everline whispered.

I hadn't heard her approach and whipped my head around to see her mouth twisted into an amused grin like she knew exactly what I'd been thinking.

"Would you like to meet my granddaughter?"

What??? The object of my fixation was Everline's granddaughter? And she'd just caught me gawking at her like some kind of stalker. How humiliating.

"Willow, sweetheart, come and meet Beck. He just moved to the area recently and started working here part time."

Willow re-shelved the book she'd been looking at then walked toward us. She moved with such grace, it was like she floated on the clouds.

I'd clearly read too many sonnets. Which was odd, as I didn't read poetry.

Smiling broadly, she held out her hand. "Hi, Beck. Nice to meet you."

My hand was sweaty. I could feel it. Should I wipe it on my pants first? Would that be too obvious? Grin and hope for the best? Her smile fell and her brows drew together as her hand hung between us without a gesture from me. Way to ruin a moment, Beck. I quickly swiped my hand on the side of my pants, then gripped hers. "Hi, Willow."

Everline looked over her shoulder as the bell over the door jingled when someone came in. "Be right with you, ladies! Staci and Bonnie are here to pick up ten copies of the next selection for their book club. Willow, since you and Beck are around the same age, I thought you could introduce him to some of your friends before school starts in a couple months. Let him get a head start." Everline turned and went to the front of the store to greet the customers, leaving me with Willow. Alone. Just the two of us.

We stood staring at each other in awkward silence for far too many moments. Say something, Beck. Anything. "I didn't know Everline had a granddaughter." Embarrassingly, my voice cracked in the middle of the sentence.

Willow tilted her head to the side and looked at me questioningly. "It was you I saw that night, wasn't it? On the deck at Joe's?"

At least one of us wasn't a blubbering idiot. She was direct. I liked it when girls were direct because it took all of the uncertainty out of the equation for me. Most of the time I didn't pick up on their social cues. Gid wasn't much better with guys. Our little brother was another story. Girls flocked around Lex all the time, and he'd long ago mastered the art of flirting. One day, I tucked my tail between my legs and asked him for help. It had been an epic disaster. After two hours, he threw up in hands in frustration and declared me a lost cause. Said the only way I'd get a girl was if she lost a bet. He did nothing to boost my confidence meter score.

"Yeah. I was waiting for my younger brother to get off work."

"Who were the other two guys?"

"My older brother and his, uh, boyfriend? Maybe?"

Her lips curved with the smallest smirk. "You don't know?"

"It's new and unlabeled," I said.

She laughed, and my stomach made a weird flippy sensation. "I get it. I have friends like that."

"Those were your friends you were with?"

She nodded.

"Do you go to Joe's often?" Smooth, Beck. Maybe ask for her zodiac sign next.

"Yeah, we do. Would you like to meet us there tonight? Maybe around seven?"

Again, I appreciated her directness. More than words could express.

"I'll be there." And just like that, my confidence meter rocketed to an all-time high.

CHAPTER SEVEN

Everline closed the bookstore on Sundays, and Dad decided to give us a rest day from major chores, so I finally had a day to myself. I knew exactly how I wanted to spend it. Bringing my arms over my head, I stretched from the tips of my fingers to my toes. Normally I'd sleep late on my day off. Even though it was a rest day, I still had some minor chores, like doing my laundry and unpacking the rest of my stuff, but it was nothing that couldn't wait a few hours. My own investigative to-do list screamed at me. I needed to check out the library—finally—to learn more about the Teller family history. Then there was the hidden room in the garage and the whole thing about a possible paranormal investigation business. Because of our busy and often conflicting work schedules, I hadn't shared my discovery and suspicions with Gid and Lex. Maybe I'd have even more to tell them if I found the history books.

I grabbed my glasses from the nightstand and put them on. A smile slid across my face as I thought about last night. I'd met Willow and her friends at Joe's. One friend brought her boyfriend, and another brought her girlfriend, so it didn't feel as awkward as it could have. At least I wasn't the only guy there, and I wasn't a fifth wheel. They were all welcoming and included me in conversations. They asked about where I'd moved from, my family, what I liked to do. The worst part of the evening was that we were seated in Lex's section, and he kept waggling his eyebrows at me when he thought no one was looking. A friend of Willow's—who was there alone and joined us for a bit—thought he was funny and asked if he was seeing anyone. Because of course she did. Girls always noticed Lex. Some guys, too. But before Aiden, he'd steered them in Gid's direction. Now he befriended them. We hadn't been in town long, but he already seemed to be pretty popular.

After dinner, I hung out on the beach for a couple hours with Willow and her friends. Someone built a fire, and we sat around it and talked. It was perfect. I didn't feel awkward or embarrass myself. Well, not very much, anyway. Willow was funny, friendly, and wicked smart. Best of all? She loved books as much as I did. Maybe she'd inherited that love from Everline, or Everline had surrounded her with books since birth and it was inevitable. We'd talked about our favorite books, must-read authors, and works we were excited about reading when they released.

She was a defender on the varsity soccer team. I admitted my lack of sports knowledge was enough to fill a chasm. She'd laughed and promised to teach me as long as I came to her games. Time passed quickly, and I'd been so comfortable around her. More comfortable than I'd ever been with Sophie. Like we'd known each other for much longer than a day. Willow offered to bring lunch by the bookstore later this week. Food from her favorite Greek restaurant. I couldn't wait.

After scrounging around on the floor for clothes—which is why I needed to do laundry—I slid on jeans, pulled a t-shirt over my head, then went downstairs to grab coffee and breakfast. For so many of us living here, it was quiet in the house. Mom texted she and Dad had taken Harper to run some errands. Lex and Gid might have been sleeping or at work. I didn't know their schedules for the day.

I appreciated the solitude. Avoiding Lex today would be a good thing. He'd tease me about last night and ask endless and no doubt stupid questions about Willow. I just wanted to keep things to myself for a while. Everything had gone so smoothly, and I didn't want to ruin that feeling.

After putting my cereal bowl and mug into the dishwasher, I headed down the hallway to the library. It had waited patiently for me for weeks now, and it was time we became acquainted. Our introduction was far overdue.

Opening the double doors to the room, I closed my eyes, breathed in deeply, and grinned from ear to ear. The smell of old books was like an aphrodisiac to me. I'd spent barely a couple minutes in here that first morning, so I took my time appreciating the details. A high ceiling gave the room an airy feeling, and towering shelves filled from top to bottom with books lined all four walls. Only the doorway I'd just entered, a few tall windows, and a stone fireplace claimed wall space free from books. An ornate wooden desk sat at one end of the room, and comfortable chairs and sofas around the fireplace begged me to spend hours in them reading. A cozy window seat filled with cushions had my name on it. Maybe I could move my bed down here. Add a fridge and a bathroom and I'd never have to leave the library.

I strolled from shelf to shelf, my hand trailing along the book spines as I explored. After browsing the first few bookcases, I silently thanked whoever had organized them by genres. It was quite a collection, and someone had taken great care of this library. Everline said Macie had been a book lover, so maybe I had her to thank. I envisioned many happy hours in my future spent here.

Something hit the hardwood floor behind me on the other side of the room, the sound like the crack of gunfire. I spun around, expecting to see Harper back early from errands with my parents grinning sneakily after following me into the library.

No one was there.

But *something* was there. A brief flash of light came then went just as quickly. Maybe it was a reflection from the morning sun shimmering through the windows. Curious, I moved to that side of the room—and felt like I'd walked into a freezer.

Weird.

I shoved my hands in my pockets. An AC vent must be close by. Then the image of the rocking chair moving on its own popped into my mind, and a shiver coiled up my spine. I wasn't sure if it was caused by the cold or the thought of the rocking chair.

Could those two things be connected?

As I briskly rubbed my arms for warmth, something on the floor caught my eye. Upon investigating, I discovered the culprit responsible for the noise. A book. A lounge chair had blocked it from my view when I was across the room. By the weathered condition of the cover and page edges, I could tell it was old. I picked it up, and then turned it over to read the tattered cover. *The Teller Family.*

I'd found it. Was there only one book? I turned my gaze to the shelves in front of me from where it must have fallen. On the top shelf was an empty slot. There's no way I could reach it, so I grabbed the rolling ladder from the corner, pulled it over, then climbed up it.

Other books with the same burgundy cover stood beside the empty slot where this one had been shelved. The first book beside the empty slot was labeled volume two of the family history. My nose tickled from the layers of dust on the shelf. Someone had clearly loved this library, but it hadn't been cleaned for quite a while.

Despite their age, the books appeared to be in fairly good condition. When I carefully opened the one in my hand, the spine cracked like it hadn't been touched in years. Inside were yellowed handwritten pages that were easily legible. People back then had far better handwriting than folks today. Mom said Harper's handwriting at age six was better than mine, Gid's, or Lex's in our teens. She wasn't wrong.

What are the odds that in this library filled with hundreds of books, the exact one I came in to find would somehow fall off the shelf on its own? It could have taken me hours if not days to locate these records. What an uncanny coincidence.

Or was it?

I shoved those puzzling and disturbing thoughts to the side with plans to revisit them later. Right now, this book called to me. I descended the ladder, strode over to the desk, then sat down to examine volume one.

Carefully turning the pages, I noted the names of my many relatives from generations past. According to this, the Tellers originated in Germany. Brothers Hans, Klaus, and Karl made their way to Scotland, where they lived for a few years. In 1835, the three brothers and their families emigrated to North Carolina and established themselves in the furniture business. Each of them had three children, and their birthdates were alongside their names.

They sure were a fertile bunch. If most of their kids had even a couple of offspring, it's easy to see how the family cemetery got so full.

After reading a few more pages, I came upon a section that listed death dates for Hans and Karl. Their causes of death weren't recorded, but in those days, it could have been from something like smallpox or tuberculosis. In fact, they'd both passed away within a year of each other. According to this, the surviving brother, Klaus, had outlived his children.

Based on the dates in this book and those on the tombstones in the cemetery, Tellers had a difficult time with longevity. My ancestors' average life expectancy fell drastically below the national average. I closed the book and set it aside to take upstairs and study later.

I retrieved the most recent volume from the shelf then settled in the window seat. Since the family had split a few generations back, I wondered if our branch of the family tree would even be mentioned. If so, would it be up to date? I flipped toward the back then gaped in surprise. There we were. My paternal grandparents, Richard and Ellen, had only one child, Joshua, my father. He married my mother Amanda twenty-two years ago and together they had us, Gideon, Beckett, Alexander, and Harper. Correct birthdates were listed for all of us, as well as the year our parents married.

Since Macie was the last of the Tellers, I guess I had her to thank for updating the book. She'd even listed Harper's information. How had she kept tabs on us all these years when we didn't even know she existed?

Wait a minute. The attorneys told Dad it took a year to track us down because no one knew where we lived. I understood the addition of my parents to the book. They'd both been born over forty years ago. But Harper was only six years old. How had Macie gotten the information? Something didn't add up.

Examining the history beyond my dad, I noted my grandfather had two siblings, a brother and sister. Both his siblings had three children. I slumped back against the cushions, pulled my glasses off and rubbed my eyes. At this rate, we might need to purchase more land to expand the cemetery. I quickly stopped myself from continuing down that morbid path.

And what was the deal with everyone having three children? Based on these books, the Tellers should be a sprawling family. I should have hordes of cousins whose names I'd be challenged to remember and family reunions requiring a convention center to fit everyone. But we truly were the last of the line.

What happened to the Tellers? I'm sure some deaths were medically related or accidents, but this many? I'd noticed several of the stones in the cemetery were for children. Far more than there should have been. I'd heard about families who were supposedly cursed, like the Kennedys and the Hemingways. Were the Tellers also on that list? I wasn't a superstitious person, but the information in these books made me want to reconsider my beliefs.

Dad and Everline had confirmed the family business was furniture manufacturing. But what about the hidden room in the garage? Newspaper clippings. EMF detectors. Other gadgets. The map with stick pins color-coded to types of spirits.

I liked to think I was more accepting of the existence of ghosts than the average person. Plenty of horror books and movies were included in my reading and watching lists. I was always open to hearing personal accounts on YouTube or television. The creepier ones had even kept me staring at dark corners in my bedroom long after I should have been sleeping.

I couldn't deny the strange things I'd uncovered over the past weeks between the cemetery, family history, and the hidden garage room. And there were the weird occurrences with my siblings. Gid hearing voices. Lex interacting with someone in his room. Harper and the lady in blue.

Harper always had a vivid imagination. Nothing would slow her down. But Gid had taken to wearing noise-cancelling headphones, and Lex tried to ignore the people he saw.

What about the rocking chair on the porch? And this book that somehow fell off a shelf on its own? Almost like someone had wanted me to find it sooner rather than hours or days later. They were saving me time. The coldness on that side of the room and the shimmer I'd seen by the window were definitely bizarre. Sure, there could be logical explanations. Maybe the sun hit my glasses in a way that produced a mysterious flash. And I still hadn't ruled out an air conditioning vent, but if one existed, it was well hidden.

I sighed heavily, not wanting to jump to illogical conclusions. Much as I tried to write off all these odd findings and events, they couldn't be ignored. Added all together, I was beginning to think we weren't alone in this house.

CHAPTER EIGHT

Between the hidden room and all it contained and the family history books and the way I'd found them, I couldn't keep all this bizarre information to myself. I needed to talk to my brothers.

Lex wasn't here, but Gid had just gotten home. After working in the garage all day, he wanted to shower before he did anything else. When I heard the water turn off, I waited about twenty minutes before I knocked on his bedroom door. He didn't answer, but I hadn't heard him go downstairs. I cracked open the door to peek inside. Just what I'd expected. He was lying on his bed in sweatpants, shirtless, his hair still wet from the shower. His eyes were closed, and his headphones were on.

Gid said those headphones were the best purchase he'd made and had worn them a lot lately. Anything to drown out the voices.

He didn't hear me when I walked in, but when I sat at the foot of the bed, he sprang up to a sitting position with a murderous look on his face. Probably thought I was Lex. I held my hands up in a surrendering motion.

He slid off the headphones.

"What's up?"

"Plenty. I made some weird discoveries over the past few days, especially in the garage. The Tellers who lived here over the years had mind-blowing secrets."

When I'd finished telling him about the hidden room and the family history books, he slumped back against his headboard and ran his hands across his face and up through his hair. "Whoa."

"Yeah."

He looked thoughtful. "If they really were paranormal investigators, how do you confirm something like that? I mean, do you have a ghostbuster kind of website or something? Advertise on the dark web? Add a coupon to a Ouija board purchase?"

I snickered at the last one. One free cleansing of whatever comes through the veil during your first séance. Not a bad gimmick.

"Maybe some people around here knew about it. Everline was friends with Macie. I could ask her."

Gid squeezed his eyes tightly shut and put his hands over his ears.

"The voices again?" I asked.

He nodded. "I dread coming home from work because at least I get relief there. Sometimes I can even block them out, but right now it's like a symphony of chainsaws is playing in my head."

"You know, maybe you should talk to Mom and Dad about this. It's been going on for a while."

"No." Gid dropped his hands and shook his head. "I know they'd do the right thing and try to get me help, but we both know they can't afford it. They're just starting to dig out from under Harp's medical bills. I'll figure it out on my own."

His response didn't surprise me. Gid had always preferred to work through things on his own. When he'd questioned his sexuality and thought he might be gay, he'd kept silent about it for months before casually tossing it out one evening at the dinner table. Last year, when his boyfriend had broken up with him, it was a month before we'd learned about it. That was only because his boyfriend was the brother of one of my friends who'd shared the information with me. Gid had really liked the guy, and I knew the breakup hurt him, but he kept everything locked inside. Lex said that's why he was a walking angry beehive. He kept all those emotions inside until the pressure was too much and the swarm escaped and stung everyone in his wake. With a vengeance. And Gid had a history of epic explosions. Maybe Aiden's chamomile tea and less caffeine remedy would help temper his explosive reactions.

That thought brought up another question. "Have you talked about it with Aiden?"

A grin tugged at his mouth. "I'd like to keep him around, so no. He might think it's too much crazy this early and then bail on me."

Gid might be grinning, but I detected a hint of pain in his eyes.

"I don't know him well, but judging by the way he looks at you, I doubt that would happen," I said.

"Well, I don't want to put him through any tests just yet." He grabbed a discarded t-shirt from the floor and pulled it over his head. "The voices aren't as loud outside, so how about you show me this secret door in the garage?"

•   •   •

Gid and I had spent the past couple of hours in the hidden room in the garage. After examining the files, we discovered each one corresponded to a color-coded pin on the maps. That was one mystery solved.

Gid stood in front of the maps. "If these are all cases the Tellers handled, seems like they'd be pretty well known in the paranormal world. I'm surprised they didn't have their own reality show." He chuckled before rapping a knuckle against the map of Louisiana. "I'd swear there was a movie about this poltergeist in New Orleans. Sure sounds familiar."

"They've been doing this for years. Some of those newspaper clippings are decades old. How do you become a paranormal investigator? Do they have schools? Online courses?" This wasn't something I'd thought about before, and all kinds of ideas ran through my mind.

"The Tellers must have passed down the work from generation to generation. I bet on-the-job training was wicked." Gid's eyes flashed with excitement and maybe even a hint of jealousy. Like he wished he'd faced the entities alongside our relatives. "Did you tell Lex yet?"

"Haven't had a chance." I picked up another file. "I took some of the family history books upstairs to study last night. Not many people ever qualified for senior citizen status."

"What about Mom and Dad? Do they know?"

I shook my head. "Can you imagine what they'd say if I told them about our relatives' other business? They'd laugh me out of the room. But the thing with so many of the family dying young... it could be a medical issue completely unrelated to the paranormal stuff. That's something we need to know. I'm thinking causes of death must be listed in the history books, and I just haven't found them yet."

Gid walked over to the shelves and examined the equipment. He picked up one of the devices, turned it over in his hands, set it down, then repeated with the next piece. As he neared the shelf holding containers of salt and jugs of liquid, I flipped through more files on the desk.

"Beck, did you notice this?"

"What?" I didn't look up.

"These jugs. The clear liquid inside is holy water."

I dropped the file on the desk then rushed over to see for myself.

"Look." He turned one so I could read its marking. "They're labeled."

I swallowed hard. Shelves full of holy water and salt. Definitely not items you find in the average home. Especially not in bulk quantities surrounded by equipment like this. I met Gid's gaze, finding his eyes open as wide as mine. "I bet these ropes aren't just regular ropes. The Tellers mentioned blessed ropes in some of the files. Are you thinking what I'm thinking?"

"This confirms it. Our relatives really were ghostbusters," he said.

"We've got to figure this out before going to Mom and Dad. We need solid proof."

· · ·

"I mean seriously, how cool is that? Did they leave us an instruction manual so we can keep the business going?" Lex had flopped on my bed right after his shower, and now his sopping wet cobalt blue hair splayed across my pillow. Probably hadn't even tried to towel dry it. He'd started to grill me about Willow just as I'd predicted. I shut him down by sharing everything I'd told Gid and what we'd found in the hidden room.

Thankfully Lex decided that information was far more interesting than giving me crap about a girl.

His reaction to the paranormal business wasn't exactly what I'd expected, but it was Lex, so I should have known better. Out of the three of us, he was always the first to try new things. Eating the weirdly shaped, brownish lump of food on his cafeteria tray that I swore moved before he stabbed it with a fork. Choosing to go down a blue slope the first time he snowboarded. It wasn't pretty. He ate a lot of snow, but he survived. He also drank the "tea" Harper made at her last party. She laughed uncontrollably after he swallowed it and then turned a greenish color. Gid and I politely declined our cups after that. We still didn't know what was in it.

"Wait, you'd want to go head-to-head with spirits? You know nothing about them. According to the clippings, some were dangerous. They even hurt people." My thoughts drifted toward the cemetery, but I forced away that line of speculation.

"You wouldn't?" Lex asked. "I bet Gid would. What did he say?"

Gid hadn't joined in on the conversation. He'd opted for sleep instead since he was exhausted from work today and was scheduled to open tomorrow morning. I remembered the excited gleam in

Gid's eyes from earlier this evening at the discoveries we'd made, but I didn't want to throw any more fuel on Lex's flame right now. He tended to go off on rambling tangents when he got excited about something and could talk in circles for hours if he wasn't stopped.

"He didn't ask about an instruction manual, okay? I'm serious, Lex. We need to figure out what's going on." Lex's eyes flitted to the far corner of my room, and he sat up abruptly, eyes wide.

"What?" I asked.

He pointed to a spot by my closet door. "Did you see that? In the corner of your room?"

"See what?" I asked, looking in the direction he pointed. All I saw was my overflowing bookshelf in the corner beside my closet door. I seriously needed more horizontal surfaces.

"Wait..." He rubbed his eyes and blinked hard. "They're gone now. I don't understand."

"Maybe I can help if you'd tell me what you saw," I said impatiently.

"There was a white flash, then two blurry forms that looked like people came out of it. They went into the hallway. You seriously didn't see?"

I leaped from the bed and poked my head outside my bedroom door, looking up and down the hallway. It was empty. I heard my parents' voices downstairs. Harper had been in bed for hours, and her door was still closed. I turned back to Lex. "There's no one out here. The hallway's empty. You're still seeing people around the house? Or what you think are people?"

"Sometimes it's only a glimpse. Like someone just went around the corner of the kitchen into the dining room. Or they turned the corner at the top of the stairs. I never see a fully formed person, but I always feel like—someone's there, you know?"

I'd noticed Lex staring over my shoulder at something—or someone—occasionally when we'd be talking. I'd assumed it was our parents walking past or Harper running through the house. After the first time he'd mentioned thinking Mom had been in his room when she wasn't, he rarely brought it up again.

"Have you ever followed them?"

"Sure. But no one's ever there. Like when I brought home that order of clams for you. I just try to ignore it. That night I thought Mom was in my room freaked me out for a while." Lex stopped to take a drink of his soda, then set the can back on my nightstand. "But I'm telling you, Beck. If I start seeing people like those creepy twin girls from *The Shining*, I'm outta here. I'll trample anyone in my way. Okay, not Harp, but I'd pick her up and carry her out the door."

"You've seen twins?"

Lex continued down a rambling path and was beyond listening to me.

"And what about that bathtub lady? Have we checked all the bathrooms and extra bedrooms in the house? Maybe those glimpses of people I'm seeing are trying to lead me to one of the rooms. I'm talking decomposed bodies, Beck. Therapy bills for a lifetime. And don't even get me started on insomnia. Once you see something like that, you can't unsee it, and it seeps into your dreams at night. Which really makes them nightmares. The infinite kind. Then you wake up screaming, cold sweat seeping from every pore of your body. And you feel the need to look under the bed, but of course you don't want to do that. Sometimes you can bring back things from your nightmares. I read a book where that happened. Sleeping becomes impossible. Do you know what days without sleep can do to a person? It's not—"

"Lex," I interrupted. He either hadn't heard me or didn't care. "Lex!" I said, raising my voice even louder as I strode across the room and kicked my mattress where he'd flopped back to the pillow during his rant.

He finally stopped talking, sat up, and stared at me, his eyes focused again. "What?"

"Don't ever let anyone say you're overdramatic." Which was a totally untrue statement. "Seriously, you need to calm down. None of this has happened."

"It could."

I tiled my head and looked at him with what had to be enormous amounts of doubt on my face. "Could it? If it makes you feel better, we'll check all the bedrooms and bathrooms tonight." I sighed heavily. "Just please don't talk about this around Harp, okay? I don't want to scare her."

"I'd never deliberately scare her. What kind of person do you think I am?"

There were so many ways to answer that question, but I wasn't taking the bait and traveling down that rabbit hole. I'd just hauled Lex out of one.

The muscles in Lex's face tightened as he clenched his jaw. "But you know I'm not making it up. I saw something. I've been seeing a lot of somethings around this house for a while now."

"I know you have, and I believe you. Gid's voices were even louder earlier this evening." I leaned against the door frame and crossed my arms. "Why isn't anything like that happening to me?"

Lex barked out a laugh. "Be glad it's not." But then he tilted his head, looking thoughtful. "Maybe it is. You felt the cold spot in the library, and a book fell off the shelf by itself. Nothing like that has happened to Gid or me."

There was also the chair that rocked by itself on the porch, something I hadn't mentioned to either of them. And possibly a lady in the cemetery the day Harper had gotten away from me.

A sudden chill enveloped the top of my shoulder, almost like someone had gently placed a hand there. I hurried out of the doorway and back toward Lex, who looked at me questioningly. "I think you might be right. It's not voices or people, but I'm experiencing something."

CHAPTER NINE

This was the first night our work schedules aligned, and Gid, Lex, and I were all home. Mom made spaghetti and meatballs, my favorite. Her sauce wasn't from a jar, and to even ask that question was a personal insult to her. It was a family recipe handed down through the generations and took two days to cook. Just thinking about it triggered my drool response. We had our first family dinner in the dining room. Lex and I volunteered to clean up while our parents took Harper out for ice cream.

I'd just finished loading the dishwasher and was headed to my room when Gid yelled. "Please stop talking!"

Strange. Lex had just taken the trash outside. Whenever Gid begged someone to stop talking, it was usually him.

"I'll do anything. Just stop." Gid moaned.

Following his voice, I found him in what Mom called the front parlor. I didn't know what that meant exactly, but it was just another room to read in if you asked me. Gid slouched on the sofa, his hands massaging his temples. He looked up as I entered the room. The dark circles beneath his eyes told the story of his sleepless nights since we'd moved in. When the three of us shared a room, Gid slept like a log. Other than the snoring. Now, a good night's sleep was a distant memory. It surprised me he hadn't fallen asleep under a car at the garage while changing the oil.

"You hear them, right?" Gid asked, a wild look in his eyes. "Tell me I'm not going crazy."

"Where are your headphones?" I asked. "Tell me and I'll get them."

"I forgot them at the garage."

"I'll drive there and pick them up."

He squeezed his eyes tightly shut and shook his head. "They're closed. I don't have a key," he said through clenched teeth.

I wanted to help him, but I didn't know how. Hearing voices in the house nearly every waking minute, especially ones that weren't attached to people, would annoy the hell out of me. He looked exhausted. It hurt to see him like this. I knew he was beyond frustrated over having no answers or solutions to his situation. I had to try something, so I sat on the chair next to him. "What are the voices saying?"

He rocked back and forth, running his hands through his hair. "It's a jumbled mess. Like I'm standing in the middle of Times Square on New Year's Eve. Voices are all around me, but nothing I can make out. This is the worst it's been. Like they're desperate for me to understand them."

Getting his headphones wasn't an option. Lex and I didn't own any, or I'd immediately hand them over to Gid. I had no idea how to make the voices stop. I felt helpless. The only thing I knew to do was try to listen harder. So, I closed my eyes and concentrated.

I opened my mind and listened to the sounds around me. The sofa squeaked lightly as Gid rocked back and forth. Wind chimes on the porch tinkled in the breeze. The back door closed as Lex came back inside. But nothing out of the...

Wait. Was that? I focused harder. There it was. A low frequency humming sound. I latched onto that hum, and it intensified to a loud buzz the longer I listened. Was this what Gid heard? It was enough to drive a person insane.

My eyes shot open. "I hear something."

Gid's head jerked up, and his gaze met mine, relief written all over his face. "You do? You hear it?"

I nodded.

His eyes narrowed. "Wait.. It's getting louder. What the..."

"You're right," I nodded. "Can you make out anything?"

He closed his eyes again, his brows drawing together in concentration. "It's a woman's voice. She's saying something about the Teller family curse?"

My heart skipped a beat, and I'm pretty sure my jaw hit the floor. With all the deaths in the family, the idea of a curse had crossed my mind, but it seemed ridiculous. To hear the words coming from Gid's lips was a shock. And yet, maybe it wasn't as much of a surprise as it should have been. "The what now? Where is the voice coming from? Can you tell?"

"Probably from that lady sitting on the sofa, idiots," Lex said, walking into the room. "You two blind or something?" He bit into the apple in his hand, then froze. His mouth dropped open, and the piece of apple in it fell to the floor along with the apple itself. It rolled across the floor and banged into the leg of my chair. "Guys, you don't see her? Then who the hell is that lady?"

"This isn't funny, Lex. There's no lady..." My head whipped around to the spot beside Gid. An older woman sat gazing back at me from where there had been an empty place just seconds ago.

I leaped from my chair and backed against the wall beside the doorway Lex had just entered. At the same time, Gid jumped over the coffee table to stand beside Lex. Or where Lex had been standing. In a botched attempt to run, he'd fallen over a footstool. Someone screamed, and I couldn't guarantee it wasn't me.

"We're all seeing her, right?" Lex asked, still on the floor as he struggled to untangle his legs. All Gid and I could do was nod, neither of us taking our eyes off the woman. The wall was the only thing keeping me upright at this point. "She's one of the people I've seen in the house. Told you I wasn't lying."

"Not really the time for I told you so, Lex." My heart raced.

The woman's hand flew to her chest, and she seemed just as shocked as we were. She wore a mint green dress and appeared to be in her mid-to-late-seventies with gray-streaked chestnut hair pulled into a loose bun at the base of her neck. A double strand of lustrous pearls, matching earrings, and a wedding ring were her only jewelry. Her widened gaze rested on each of us briefly, then her body slumped forward as if she was relieved.

I'm sure our expressions would have been comical in another setting, but this lady had appeared out of thin air. I'd be the first to admit there was no shortage of strange occurrences in this house, but this had to be the weirdest.

"Who are you?" I asked, my voice wavering. She looked strangely familiar to me

She clasped her hands together in her lap. "I'm Macie, your distant cousin. Technically, your cousin by marriage." Her voice was kind and patient, but it did nothing to calm my racing pulse.

Lex had finally separated himself from the footstool. He now stood beside Gid but kept his distance. "No way. Macie's dead. And you don't look like a ghost. You're as solid as us, like you're a live person."

I noted the wrinkles in her skirt and the laugh lines at her eyes and mouth, but there was no indentation on the sofa where Macie sat. Uncanny.

"Well, yes, I am dead." She smoothed her dress over her knees. "But like many others in our family, I'm trapped here."

Strike the earlier remark about the weirdest occurrence. This revelation topped it. If what she said was true, the ghosts of our dead relatives roamed the house. Which explained what Lex had been seeing all along. The part of my brain that wasn't still in shock tried and failed to rationalize what was happening right now.

"She's not lying, Lex. This is Macie. I've seen her picture in the family history books from the library and on the wall in the hallway upstairs." I'd also seen her grave in the cemetery. Reconciling the image of her rotting corpse in the coffin with the elegant lady who sat in front of me wasn't a simple task.

Gid's brows drew into a straight line and understanding dawned on him. "All that chatter and noise in my head. It was you and… whatever else is in the house."

Macie nodded. "Yes. We've been trying to get your attention for so long. The three of you needed to be together, but that's easier said than done. Tonight is the first time it's happened since you moved in, but I didn't want to interrupt your family dinner. You're such busy boys."

Gid seemed to have overcome his shock and moved in front of Lex and me, making himself a barrier between us and Macie. With his broad shoulders tensed and jaw clenched, he was a bundle of coiled energy. And not the good kind. The angry vibes he gave off made people want to steer clear of him. I'd seen mothers grab their children's hands and lead them in a direction that wouldn't cross paths with Gid. Lex claimed he was the reason Gid hadn't been arrested for going off on someone. His provocations allowed Gid to release the gradual buildup of tension and he felt slighted no one had acknowledged this contribution and shown their gratitude, something he'd mentioned more than once while I struggled to hold Gid back from pounding him.

Her gaze turned to Lex. "You could see me and others?"

"Mostly just you." Lex crossed his arms over his chest and tilted his head in challenge. He'd grown braver since toppling over the footstool. "Question. You won't try to possess one of us so you can live again, right? It would be just plain weird having an old woman controlling my body."

Gid and I stared at him.

He shrugged. "What? I'm the one asking the hard questions here. You guys should thank me for trying to keep you alive."

Macie's mouth quirked into a half smile. "Um, no. You can keep your bodies to yourselves." She turned in my direction. "Gid can hear me, and Lex can see me. What about you?"

Lex and I discussed this the other night, and I'd wondered the same thing. What about me? I believed I'd felt their presence and heard a low buzzing a few minutes ago when I really concentrated. So how did I figure into this ghost equation? My brothers had seen and heard things for weeks. Gid and I talked about it on the porch that night I'd seen the rocking chair move on its own. Just a couple of nights ago, Lex saw figures leave my bedroom and go into the hallway.

Then something clicked. Gid didn't hear the voices clearly or see Macie, and Lex only caught glimpses of people, but never heard the chatter until we were all together in the same room. Macie said the three of us needed to be together. Did I have something to do with that?

"I have an idea." I turned and stepped out of the room, waiting just around the corner.

"What the... where did she go?" Gid asked.

"She's sitting on the sofa in the same place," Lex replied.

"Gah! That insane buzzing is back. Beck, get back in here," Gid growled.

The second my foot crossed the threshold, we all saw and heard Macie again. Somehow, it took the three of us together for her to be visible and communicate. As if I enhanced my brothers' abilities.

"Weird," Lex said.

Gid growled, but he'd lowered his guard. Macie didn't appear to be a threat to us. She was a nice, older lady who just happened to be a ghost. Then again, the spirit that came out of the Ark of the Covenant in the first Indiana Jones movie seemed peaceful at first. But look what happened to the guys who didn't close their eyes. Faces melting off bones was no joke and not to be taken lightly.

"I seem to be the conduit that makes the spirits obvious to the rest of us. The bigger questions are *why* we have these abilities, and why you and other family members are in this house? Shouldn't you have moved on or gone to the light or whatever happens after death?"

"I can explain the abilities, but other issues are more important. I'm afraid you've inherited more than just this house. You need to know about the Teller family curse," Macie said. And then she blinked out of sight as if she'd never been there at all.

CHAPTER TEN

"Where did…" Gid started as he turned around the room searching for Macie.

"Curse? We're cursed. Fantastic." Lex dropped his hands to his sides with a loud slap. "But maybe some of us are more cursed than others. That could happen, right?"

"Would you two shut up?" I interrupted.

"You're not supposed to say shut up," Harper said. "What are you doing?"

We spun in her direction. She stood in the doorway, hands on her hips, and stared up at us with an inquisitive look.

"Hey, Harp," I said, trying to calm my voice. "How long have you been standing there?"

"I don't know. I'm bored, and Mom's unpacking again." She rolled her eyes. "Want to play a game?"

The three of us exchanged relieved glances. Harper hadn't seen Macie. I didn't know how we'd have handled that situation. She might not have been able to see or hear Macie, anyway. Just one more thing to add to the list of "Stuff We Didn't Know" that continued to grow.

Lex held out his hand. "Come on. I challenge you to a game of checkers. And no getting Rex to help you this time."

Harper's eyes brightened as she took Lex's hand and tugged him toward the door. "I love checkers! It's always so easy to beat you."

Lex turned to look at Gid and me over his shoulder and mouthed, "Figure this out."

I raked my hand through my unruly hair. "That was close."

"Why do you think Macie disappeared?"

"Could be plenty of reasons. She said it's only possible to communicate with us if all three of us are together. This is new and unknown, so we might have done something wrong that made her leave—energy or vibes, I don't know. She's a ghost. Maybe she can only be corporeal for a certain amount of time."

Gid shrugged. "She seems like a nice grandma. Maybe she knew Harp was coming and didn't want to scare a little girl."

"Macie never got to be a grandma," I said. "She and Everline were friends. She said Macie's daughter died at the age of ten, she lost both of her sons on the same day when they were in their twenties, and her husband died somewhere between the kids' deaths. She lived alone in this house for years."

"That's so horrible," Gid said quietly, his gaze unfocused as he stared at the wall.

His thoughts were probably similar to mine. Our parents would be destroyed if they lost any of us, let alone all of us. "So, what do we do now? Any idea what this curse is?"

Remembering so many identical death dates on tombstones in the family cemetery and the sprawling family tree that only had six members left, I replied, "Yeah, I just might. I need to check some things."

•   •   •

I had questions. Lots of them. And I had a feeling Everline knew more about what went on in that house than she'd said. Secrets she was keeping for Macie. Or maybe secrets Macie revealed to her that Everline had no idea what to do with. Stories that sounded so outlandish she didn't believe them. But Everline had known her for years, and I'd bet there was more to their conversations during book deliveries than just an exchange of money and a glass of iced tea.

I wasn't scheduled to work until the store opened in another hour, but I knew Everline always came in early. Without customers in the store, we'd have privacy and time to talk. My brothers and I desperately needed to know what was happening. Why the Tellers were cursed. Why there were ghosts living in our house. Technically, maybe it was still their house. But why couldn't they cross over and rest in peace?

Then there were my parents. What the heck were we supposed to tell them? Did Dad have any idea about this other branch of the family and their paranormal business? Could he see or hear the ghosts, too? Getting answers to even a couple of these questions might tell me where to go from here.

Using my key, I unlocked the front door of the store and then locked it behind me. I'd learned that die-hard booklovers would try to get inside the second they saw an employee enter. I sympathized with them. I'd waited in line on book release days, anxious to get my hands on a highly anticipated novel and start reading. Trying to shoulder my way in a little earlier wasn't beneath me, and I'd attempted it more than once.

Everline sat at the desk in her office working on the computer. Her gaze met mine over her reading glasses as I entered the room. "Beck, I'm surprised to see you here so early. You're not scheduled for another hour. Did you misread the schedule?"

Mr. Darcy sat on the edge of her desk, and I scratched under his chin before taking a seat. "No, but I was hoping we could talk about some things before we opened. Namely, my extended family."

Her brows raised in question.

"I met Macie."

Everline took off her reading glasses, blinked slowly, then sat back in her chair. "Now that's a statement I didn't expect. Did you say you met Macie?"

I nodded.

"But that's impossible. She's dead."

"Yes, she is." I tilted my head and met her gaze. "But you don't seem all that surprised by what I said. Are you telling me there's no way my brothers and I could have met Macie even though she's buried in the family cemetery? I've seen her grave. You mentioned being in that house made you uncomfortable. I think you're not telling me everything you know."

Everline stared at me for a long moment. Mr. Darcy hopped from the desk onto my lap, kneaded my leg, then curled up for a nap. "I'm not denying a person's remains could be in one place while their spirit is in another. I knew the second I stepped over the threshold that house wasn't normal. Macie's revelations confirmed it."

"The Teller family furniture business was legit. I've seen the old factory and clearly, they did well for themselves. But I've found things that make me believe it wasn't their only business. Do you know anything about that?"

Everline inhaled deeply and released a long breath. "The deaths of Macie's sons weren't the result of a mishap in the factory. As far as the public knows, a tragic accident happened after hours while they were repairing machinery. How much do you know?"

I pushed my glasses up my nose with one hand while I ran my fingers through Mr. Darcy's fur with the other. "Judging by what I found in a secret room in the garage, it has something to do with the paranormal. Ghosts, demons, poltergeists maybe? There were files, notes, and newspaper clippings from all over the country going back decades."

Everline gazed at a spot on the wall for a moment, eyes unfocused as if she was reliving a memory. "That would go along with what Macie told me. Some of her stories were so bizarre, like something you'd see in movies or read in books. She spoke of her relatives trapping poltergeists and helping spirits cross over to the next realm. Even sending demons back to hell. I didn't know what to believe. Were they the ramblings of a woman who'd lived alone in a big house for too long? Were the stories real? Any sane person would question their authenticity." She leaned forward and rested her hands on the desk in front of her. "One thing I never doubted was her fear. Macie was scared something would happen to her. She was also terrified for your family."

My hand froze on Mr. Darcy's black fur. "I found our names and birthdates in the family history book, so she knew about us. Why did it take her attorneys a year to locate Dad?"

"She knew exactly where you were. Private investigators kept up with you for quite a while. Macie instructed her attorneys to wait a year after her death to contact you," Everline replied. She shook her head slowly. "I certainly don't claim to understand everything that happened to the Tellers, but I know there's no one left to recite the tale. That family cemetery is bursting at the seams, and a lot of Teller parents, including Macie, outlived their children. As a parent myself, that's a fate I wouldn't wish on anyone." Everline's gaze dropped to the desk, and her eyes glistened with tears. I wasn't sure if her sadness was for Macie, or if she'd suffered a loss herself. I didn't want to overstep my bounds and ask such a personal question. Maybe she'd share that information with me at some point, or maybe not. It was her choice.

Mr. Darcy popped his head up a second before someone entered the back door.

"Grandma? I brought croissants."

A smile lit up my face when I saw who it was.

Willow's long curls were pulled back into a ponytail, but a few strands had come loose and fallen around her face. My fingers itched to tuck them behind her ears. She carried a bag from The Bun Also Rises, a bakery located a few doors down from the bookstore. The play on the Hemingway novel title had immediately caught my attention, and I'd wanted to check out the bakery based on the name alone. The smell emanating from the bag was heavenly. I'd eaten breakfast just a half hour ago, but that didn't stop my mouth from watering.

Everline discreetly wiped her tears away. "Good morning, sweetheart," she said, pulling her granddaughter into a side hug.

Willow smiled broadly when she noticed me. Mr. Darcy jumped from my lap to the desk to sniff the bakery bag. He must have thought it smelled as good as I did.

"Hi, Beck," Willow said brightly. "Do you like croissants? I have extra. You've got to try these. They're stuffed with hazelnut cream. Absolutely addictive."

In the short time I'd known Willow, I learned she had a weakness for baked goods and desserts. The day she'd brought lunch from her favorite Greek restaurant was the first time I'd tried baklava. How I'd allowed myself to be deprived of it for so long was a tragic oversight on my part.

"Sure, I'll try one. Thanks, Willow. I've been meaning to stop by that bakery."

"Don't you just love the name? When it opened, I immediately wanted to go there just because of it."

I smiled because her thoughts so closely echoed my own.

She passed out napkins, then pulled a flaky croissant from the bag and placed it in front of me. "I bet you'll love it."

"My girl knows her baked goods, Beck. She's dropped by with these at least a few mornings every week this summer since the bakery opened. Not that I need them." Everline patted her stomach before taking a bite.

It took about two seconds after biting into mine before my eyes rolled back into my head, and I knew The Bun Also Rises was now a daily routine stop before work. The croissant was delicate and fluffy, and the hazelnut cream inside addictive just as Willow said. It was even better than Mom's family recipe for waffles that had been passed down from her great grandmother. But I'd never share that with her.

"By that groan, I'm guessing you like it." Willow grinned.

My cheeks flushed in embarrassment. I hadn't noticed I'd groaned out loud. Picking up the napkin, I wiped my mouth before answering. "This is amazing. If I keep eating these, I'll have to add a few more miles to my runs."

"Oh! I meant to ask if you wanted to run on the beach this evening. Soccer practice starts in a few weeks, so I might as well get a head start on training," Willow said.

Did I want to run with Willow? More than I could possibly say. I'd even dreamed about the two of us on the beach—but we hadn't been running. A detail I'd omit. "Sure. After work I'll go home and change then meet you on the sand."

Everline rose from the chair and threw her trash away. "Guess I'd better unlock the door and get to work."

"I'll be right there, Everline," I called before turning to Willow. She'd started picking up discarded napkins and wiping crumbs from the desk. "See you later?"

"Absolutely," she said, then kissed me on the cheek before leaving out the back door.

When I went to Everline to get my assignments for the day, my eyes a tad unfocused and a goofy smile plastered across my face, her knowing glance told me she knew exactly who'd put it there.

• • •

How did you tell your parents they'd inherited not only a ghost-infested house but also a family curse? And by the way, your three sons can hear and see the aforementioned ghosts. That's not a topic of conversation I'd seen covered before. Not even on all the crappy daytime talk shows. Lex suggested Googling it. I told him if he thought it would be beneficial to go ahead. He'd shrugged, then fixed himself a turkey sandwich instead. Gid was no help. When it came to conducting calm, rational discussions, he was the last name on our list.

And that was even after Harper.

An opportunity came about the next evening when my brothers and I were all home. Harp went to bed early after a day of swimming at the beach, and our parents were sharing a bottle of wine on the patio.

Before we went outside, I double checked Harper was sleeping. It wouldn't be the first time she'd faked sleep to eavesdrop on the adults. She was so stealthy that it took all of us a while to catch on. When Harper started mentioning things in conversations she couldn't possibly know, there was only one way she could have found out. Mom questioned her about listening in on other people's conversations, but Harper denied everything. She's a gutsy kid, and we couldn't take the rap for her on this one. After years with us, Mom was a pro at interrogation and finally wore her down. To Harp's credit, she almost broke Lex's record in holding out.

If you asked me, she hadn't learned her lesson and was still eavesdropping. We just hadn't caught her yet.

Mom and Dad sat on a patio sofa, a wine bottle open on the table in front of them. They shared a laugh, looking more relaxed than I'd seen them in quite a while. Guilt settled in. I hated we were about to spoil their evening. Maybe even their lives.

Dad looked up as we approached. "You boys have plans tonight? Going out somewhere?"

"Or maybe you have a date?" Mom asked, giving Gid a knowing side eye.

His face flushed a scarlet color.

"No." Gid said. The rest was mumbled and unintelligible. The thing with Aiden was still new, and Gid had always felt awkward talking to our parents about anyone he'd dated. He held things close to the vest.

I hadn't mentioned Willow to my parents yet. Mom would be on me to ask her over for dinner if I did. She'd been hoping Gid would ask Aiden, too. If it ever happened, we'd have to make sure it was on an evening when Lex was scheduled to work. He'd never make it through a meal without embarrassing us, Aiden, or Willow. Gid and I were used to it.

At our last house, we'd been in the middle of dinner the night after Gid had a first date with the guy who'd eventually broken his heart. Mom asked if the date had gone well. Lex made googly eyes and asked if he'd set Gid's heart on fire. Rolls flew across the table, insults were hurled, and I'd covered Harper's ears before she heard the worst of the language.

There was no need for Aiden and Willow to suffer, too.

We each took a seat across from our parents. As usual, they'd elected me to lead the conversation. "We need to talk to you about something. It's going to sound pretty crazy..."

"This takes crazy to a whole new level," Lex interrupted.

Gid glared at him in response.

I decided to ease my way into this. "Have either of you noticed anything unusual in the house since we moved in?"

They looked at us in concern.

"You mean besides the spider webs, mouse droppings, and heaping mounds of hoarded items?" Mom asked.

Were any ghosts listening? Would they take offense to the implication they were hoarders? Gid, Lex, and I were together, but from what I could tell, we were alone out here at the moment. I hoped none of our ancestors were eavesdropping.

I shook my head. "No, more like we aren't exactly alone in the house. And that doesn't include the critters."

"What do you mean?" Dad asked, puzzled. "You've seen someone in the house?"

"He means we're sharing our home with generations of dead Tellers," Lex said. "They roam about the rooms and grounds freely. Trust me, we're far outnumbered."

I face planted into my hand. Why hadn't we gagged him before starting this conversation?

"What?" Mom's voice rose nervously.

I sighed. "That's not the way I'd have told you, but he's not joking. When we first moved in, Lex saw glimpses of people who couldn't possibly be there. Gid heard voices almost nonstop. When the three of us are together, I'm kind of like an amplifier, and we can all see and hear them."

Dad's face reddened in agitation. "Is this some kind of joke? Why would you make up a ridiculous story like this?"

"I promise, we're not making it up, Dad. We've even spoken to Macie, the woman we inherited the house from."

Mom shook her head. "That's absurd. Someone is obviously playing a joke on you, and it's not amusing at all."

Gid, Lex, and I shared a glance. How could we convince them? Short of producing a ghost right here in front of them, I was out of ideas. Would they even be able to see the spirit with us present? That's something we'd have to try.

"I promise you, Mom, no one is playing a joke on us, and we're not pranking you and Dad. We've all seen Macie, and she's not dangerous. She wanted to share some important family history, but disappeared before she could tell us. We want to try and bring her back."

Dad crossed an ankle over his knee and draped his arm over the back of the patio sofa. "So, the house is haunted, there are family secrets I need to know, and the three of you communicate with ghosts like they're neighbors we've invited over for dinner."

"Except they were here first," Lex said.

Gid looked at him in disdain. "You just can't help yourself, can you?"

Lex shrugged. "Some things just need to be said."

"I'm not a believer. More like a skeptic." Dad was silent for a long moment as if weighing the situation before he spoke. This wasn't something as simple as spotting us some gas money or borrowing his car. He was basically being asked to participate in a pseudo-séance. Not your everyday request. "Okay. I'll give you boys the benefit of the doubt. When can we meet with Macie?"

I looked at Mom. "We were counting on you to stay with Harp and make sure she doesn't eavesdrop again. I don't want her to be scared for no reason. Then Dad can catch you up." The two of them looked at each other and silently communicated in the way couples do when they'd been together for years. I hoped I was around long enough to have that with someone one day. The lifespans of our relatives weren't encouraging.

Dad swiveled back to face us. "Okay. Tomorrow evening?"

I nodded.

"I've got a feeling time isn't on our side," Lex said before opening the back door and stepping inside.

Gid said nothing. Not even a growl.

We both knew Lex was right.

CHAPTER ELEVEN

Our parents leaned toward there being a practical explanation for what we had been experiencing. They weren't die-hard skeptics, but they certainly bent in that direction. At least Dad did. After further questioning, we learned neither of them had experienced anything remotely out of the ordinary since we'd moved in.

Mom would be easier to convince. She swore when she was eight she'd seen the ghost of her grandmother a few hours after she'd died. She'd laid a hand on Mom's shoulder and smiled at her, almost as if she was saying goodbye. Because of that, Mom considered herself more sensitive to the paranormal. I got the impression she felt slighted since none of the spirits had reached out to her here. She kind of took it personally.

But at least she and Dad were willing to believe us. Well, she was closer to believing. For Dad, it was more of a "believe it when I see it" kind of thing.

The next evening, Dad went into the parlor where Macie had first appeared with the three of us. Mom kept Harper occupied upstairs with some kind of craft project. The last thing we needed was her hearing stories about ghosts that could give her nightmares. Let alone seeing any ghosts living—really unliving, I guess—in the house with us. She'd never sleep in her own bed again.

Gid and I took the same seats we'd been in the night Macie had appeared, and Dad sat on the sofa facing Gid. Because of Lex's less than successful attempt to run away from Macie that evening, he'd moved the offending footstool to the corner and sat beside Dad. His actions that night, combined with his prior statement that it would be fun to meet a ghost, guaranteed hours of entertainment for Gid and me. We planned to bring it up at least a few times per month. Or week.

Dad looked down at the coffee table, then back at Gid and me questioningly. "Do you need a Ouija board to communicate with her?"

"A Ouija board? Seriously?" Lex asked in an insulted tone. "We're far more advanced than that. Tell him, Beck."

Dad turned to me with an expectant look on his face. "Alone, none of us can communicate with the spirits. Gid hears their voices, Lex sees them, and I seem to open the channels. When I'm around, all three of us can see, hear, and talk with Macie. She didn't stay long when we saw her. We're not sure if that was because of her energy, ours, or something else." I pushed my glasses up my nose. "It's all new to us, so we're still trying to figure things out. But she mentioned a Teller family curse and before she could explain, she disappeared."

"A Teller family curse," Dad repeated. He did a poor job of hiding a subtle smirk, even though he covered his mouth. He still wasn't on board the paranormal train yet. "I've heard nothing about a curse, but surely it couldn't be as bad as you think." He managed to assume a reassuring voice. "There's got to be an explanation."

"Everline said Macie knew where we were, but insisted her attorneys wait a year before contacting you. She thinks it might be connected," I said.

"Have you toured the family cemetery?" Lex asked Dad. "It's full of dead Tellers. You've already lived longer than a lot of our relatives."

Gid's knee bounced nervously. "Can we get started? How do we summon her?"

"Summon? I don't really care for that word." Macie appeared on the sofa beside Gid just as she had before, looking regal in the mint green dress and pearls she wore the last time. I guessed it was the outfit they'd buried her in. Macie looked directly at Dad, a gentle smile on her face. "Hello, Joshua. It's a pleasure to meet you finally."

Dad's face paled, but at least he didn't entangle himself in furniture like Lex did. He shifted uncomfortably but spoke to her. "Uh, yes, nice to meet you also, Macie."

"I realize this must be a shock for you. Your sons handled it fairly well, all things considered."

Crimson inched up Lex's face when Macie glanced briefly at him.

She continued in a hurried, desperate tone. "There are important things your family needs to know as soon as possible. I'm not sure how much time we'll have before she makes herself known."

"She?" Dad asked.

"I've watched Beck studying the graves in the family cemetery, comparing dates and researching the family tree." She cut her eyes in my direction. "Those family history books didn't fall off the shelf by accident."

So I'd been correct in thinking I wasn't alone in the library that day.

"There's a reason so many of our relatives died young, Joshua. And her name is Cora Annison."

"I don't understand." I leaned forward and propped my elbows on my knees. "You're telling me all these deaths are due to one person? But it's been going on for over a century."

Macie held her hand up in a placating gesture. "I know you have questions, but I'm not sure how long I'll be able to stay with you. My energy isn't limitless. As the three of you become stronger, I'm able to share that strength and remain corporeal. Now that you understand how to communicate with us, it will get easier." She smoothed her dress over her knees, something she'd probably done countless times when living.

"I'll tell you the story the way it was told to me. We'll worry about questions later, okay?" Macie met all our gazes briefly as each of us nodded.

If I wanted to live past my twentieth birthday, hearing about this curse was the priority right now.

"Furniture isn't the only way the Tellers made money. Starting in Germany in the mid-1800s, brothers Karl, Klaus, and Hans made a name for themselves in the paranormal world as a side business. They debunked mediums, investigated hauntings, things of that nature." She waved a hand. "Word of their success spread, and they were called to Scotland for a troublesome case. After tripping and falling off a sidewalk into the path of an oncoming carriage, a ten-year-old child named Iona died from her injuries in front of her school. Her spirit lingered, angry at her life being cut so short. Her death was an accident, but she blamed the other students for her fall. She haunted the school she'd attended, scaring the students and hurting both them and the teachers. Some of her antics even resulted in deaths. Iona's mother, Cora, was so distraught over her daughter's passing, she ended her own life so she could be with her child.

"Most spirits move on to the next realm after death. But if someone has unfinished business, they remain on this plane. One service the brothers offered was helping those lingering souls move on. They used ancient, blessed daggers engraved with various symbols and three different gems at the tip of the hilts. A ruby representing vitality, strength, and courage. An amethyst to banish and ward off spirits. And a sapphire for peace, wisdom, and clarity.

"When Cora realized the brothers planned to take her child from her again, she begged and pleaded for Iona to be spared. But Iona was responsible for the deaths of many children, and she'd only grown more aggressive. The brothers had no other option. After her daughter was gone, Cora seethed with rage and swore revenge. She cursed every descendent of Hans, Karl, and Klaus, vowing to end the Teller line. Except for your family, she's succeeded. In addition, she also cursed the descendants to remain in this plane. None of us is at peace."

The room was oppressive with silence and probably a little disbelief. A centuries old family curse that took out one's entire family was a heavy burden to drop in the span of ten minutes. Definitely not on the list of typical family problems.

Lex spoke first because of course he would. "Since it's taken so long, I'd guess she enjoys playing with her food."

"Yes, she does," Macie agreed. "The brothers put little stock in Cora's curse, but after the sudden deaths of two of their children, they decided not to take any chances. They moved their families to North Carolina, with Klaus eventually settling into this house. Believing they'd left Cora behind, they went on with their lives and started the furniture company. Before long, they returned to the paranormal business and word of their success spread. Calls came in from all over the country."

"If they left Cora behind in Scotland, how did she get here? I mean, can spirits travel? Especially that far?" I asked.

"They always believed Cora attached herself to one brother. That way, there was no chance she'd lose their location. She was dormant for several years after they arrived in North Carolina, during which time the family grew, but it wasn't long before she started picking them off one by one."

Dad's pale skin now had a grayish tint to it. It couldn't be easy hearing some evil spirit hell-bent on revenge was coming after his sons. And probably him. He cleared his throat. "So you're asking me to take a giant leap of faith and believe a woman from Scotland who died over one hundred years ago has lingered in this plane as a spirit while cursing our entire family and sending them all to early graves?"

She smoothed her skirt. "Not to mention preventing our souls from moving on."

"How does that even happen?" Dad leaped to his feet and started pacing. Now I knew where Gid got it from. "How can you be sure it was Cora? Surely the deaths were coincidental and caused by something else, right? Car accidents, heart attacks, or diseases?"

"Lex is correct when he said you should visit the family cemetery, Joshua," Macie suggested gently. "A high number of deaths occurred the same day. Some people died in very gruesome ways."

"As far as I know, my side of the family was never involved in the paranormal business," Dad said. "That may be the reason for the split a few generations back. So why us? We did nothing to her."

"Many family members who weren't connected to the paranormal business died under mysterious circumstances. Some even in your line."

My grandfather died suddenly in his early sixties from a heart attack. It was one reason Dad kept a religious workout schedule. Heart attacks weren't uncommon, but Poppy hadn't had any risk factors or family history, and his death came as a shock. My great grandfather was killed in a freak accident when a wooden beam in his barn fell on top of him. Kind of made me wonder now.

"Didn't any of the Tellers ever seek outside help? You mentioned they traveled across the country dealing with paranormal phenomena. Surely they weren't the only people in the business," Dad said.

He made a good point, and it was something I hadn't considered. There was no shortage of ghost hunter footage on TV or social media, so there had to be other options.

Macie nodded. "There's a family in New Orleans, the Broussards, who've been in the business for decades. Some of them traveled here about thirty years ago, but when they started experiencing near death situations, our family advised them to leave. They didn't want anyone else to die.

"Other than that, Cora focused primarily on this branch of the family to end the line. I wasn't a blood relation, but she toyed with me for years after the deaths of my sons and daughter." She paused a moment at the mention of her children. Losing a child was probably a pain that never lessened. Even in the afterlife. "Over the years, I kept tabs on your side of the family with the help of a private investigator. Before my death, I asked the attorneys to wait a year before contacting you. I'd hoped Cora would grow weary of her revenge. Perhaps think she'd succeeded in ending the line. I wasn't certain she was even aware of your family's existence. I dearly hoped she'd have crossed over and the rest of us could find our way, too."

"Maybe she has," I said. "Nothing's happened. She hasn't threatened us, and we're still alive. Maybe she moved on."

Macie shook her head sympathetically. "I'm sorry, Beck, but she's still here. All of us on the other side of the veil feel her venomous presence. I suspect she hasn't shown herself yet because she's watching, waiting to see how strong you are. No one's fought her for years. Some generations of siblings have been stronger than others, but none have been able to vanquish her. And apparently her thirst for revenge hasn't been quenched."

"What do you mean stronger?" Gid asked. "You said my brothers and I had to be together for us to see the spirits. What does that mean?"

"Spirits can gift humans with supernatural abilities, and that's what I and other Tellers have done for you, Beck, and Lex. We wanted to give you any advantage we could. That's why you're able to communicate with us. I guess it took a while for the abilities to kick in, but now they'll only grow stronger. Soon you'll be able to see and converse with us on your own. From what I understand, Hans, Klaus, and Karl had certain abilities that aided them in their paranormal business. They were tied to the daggers I mentioned earlier."

"So, they had abilities but still died. You're saying it's hopeless and there's nothing we can do." Dad, looking grief stricken, leaned heavily against the back of the sofa. "Cora will kill me and my sons."

Macie shook her head. "Not exactly. You have options. There's hope. If you look back through the family tree, there were always three siblings to battle Cora. Even on your branch, Joshua, there were always three children. I was very surprised to learn you're an only child."

Dad cleared his throat. He grasped his hands so tightly that his knuckles were white. "My mother had two still births before me. I was their miracle baby."

My eyes widened in surprise. Dad had never mentioned this, but I guess he'd never had a reason to. I thought about my Nonna being pregnant for so many months, feeling the baby move, and all the plans she and Poppy must have made. And then two of their children didn't survive past birth. So much death, sadness, and grief in this family. At least they finally had Dad and were able to watch him grow and then meet three of his children before they'd passed.

"Why three?" Gid asked.

"Throughout human history, the number three has always had a unique significance in religion, mysticism, and superstition. It represents balance, completeness, and harmony. If three forces come together, they can generate a greater impact or achieve a desired outcome. The most stable geometric shape is a triangle. All of this began with three brothers, and every generation after produced three siblings. I can't speculate why, but maybe it's nature's way of trying to eradicate evil. The paranormal world is full of oddities that offer no explanation.

"Harper is the only fourth sibling I'm aware of in any branch of the family tree. Every generation produced only three children. Some tried for more, some less, and others none at all. But no matter what, there were always three. I'm not sure of the significance of that, but it makes me wonder if one of you is hurt or killed, she'll be required to take your place."

My heart stuttered at her words, and I felt a cold sweat trickle down the nape of my neck. I heard Macie's words about the number three as if I were in a tunnel. It was what she'd said after that grabbed me. "One of us would die? Harper would have to fight Cora?"

Macie's gaze met mine. "I might be wrong, and I hope I am."

My heart hammered in my ears. Dad's head dropped in defeat. Lex's eyes widened in horror.

Gid leaped to his feet, his hands clenching and unclenching. "No. No way. She'll never touch Harp." He began pacing the floor, running his hands through his hair in frustration and fear.

Lex looked at Macie, his lip quivering slightly. "She wouldn't hurt Harper, would she? She's just a little girl."

"I've studied the books, Lex," I said. "Cora's never left a sibling alive. The cemetery isn't just made up of adult graves. Plenty of kids are there, too. Harper wouldn't be the youngest Cora struck down."

Macie's tone was kind but firm. "As Beck said, she wouldn't be the first child Cora has hurt. Hans, Karl, and Klaus separated her from her own young daughter, so the circumstances are the same in her eyes. She took my daughter Emily when she was only ten years old."

Gid stopped pacing and faced us. "Then we can't fail. The three of us will survive for Harper. Whatever it takes."

Dad raised his head, his expression anguished and eyes watering. "A father should never have to choose between his children, and I refuse to. I can't lose any of you. I won't." He turned to Macie. "Isn't there anything I can do? Can't I take their places and deal with her myself?"

Macie's expression was full of sympathy. "I'm sorry, Joshua, that's not the way it works. You must have three siblings standing against her to have a chance at defeating her once and for all."

"But how are we supposed to do that?" I asked. "There's a cemetery full of family that she's murdered for over a century. What makes us any different?"

"We don't even have the paranormal training the rest of them had," Lex added.

"Is there even a chance?" Gid asked.

"Possibly," Macie replied.

"Possibly isn't good enough," Gid growled.

I held my hand up in a stopping motion for him to hold his comments. "What is it, Macie? We're willing to try anything."

"My sons had a theory about the daggers that were originally used by Hans, Karl, and Klaus to kill ghosts in Germany, Scotland, and in this country. Each was engraved with various runes designed to disrupt a spirit's energy. Supposedly, the daggers can steal that energy and absorb it into the blades. It increases the power of the daggers."

"So, the more ghosts killed, the more powerful the daggers, the easier it is to trap them?" Lex asked.

"Theoretically," Macie replied.

Gid threw up his hands in exasperation. "First you said there's hope, then you said we could possibly win, and now you're saying theoretically the daggers can help us. So which is it? I'm tired of all these half answers. If the daggers can help us kill Cora, then tell us where they are so we can put an end to this Teller curse and save our family."

If ghosts breathed, it looked as if Macie sighed heavily. "It's not that simple, Gid. When some spirits die, their souls are finally at peace, and they move on to the next world or wherever they go. Others aren't that easy. Some ghosts are so filled with rage at what happened to them they can't accept they're dead. Even after being stabbed with the daggers, their souls can be drawn into them and trapped inside. There are documented instances in the family history book."

We just couldn't catch a break. The daggers could help break the curse, but they may also contain angry spirits. "Could the spirit hurt the wielder of the dagger?"

"It's possible, I suppose. There are options out there to help protect them. Psychic shielding and amulets and talismans are just a few."

"Great, so you can teach us about ways to protect ourselves." Gid stopped pacing long enough to lean on the back of Lex's chair. "Tell us where the daggers are, and we can get started."

Macie pulled at her dress hem again. "That brings me to the next problem. No one has seen the daggers for nearly one hundred years."

Gid growled loudly, turned toward the window, and ran his hands through his hair again. Lex looked as if he was on the verge of bursting into laughter. Probably because the odds against us defeating Cora kept climbing, and he dealt with stressful situations by using humor. Dad's expression remained forlorn, as if his entire world had just crashed into pieces around him.

"What happened to them? Wouldn't that be the primary weapon in defeating Cora? I mean, something that important wasn't accidentally misplaced, right?"

"Not misplaced, Beck. Hidden by someone in the family. Remember what I said about spirits being trapped inside the daggers?"

I nodded.

"Cora's daughter, Iona, is one of them. Cora wants more than anything to be reunited with her daughter. Until that happens, she'll continue to kill Tellers and see the curse through to its end."

"How does this revenge-fueled uber assassin think we'd be able to bring her daughter back?" Lex asked. "And I'd like to add that Iona dividing her soul into three objects is a very Voldemort thing to do."

Gid cast a dark glance at Lex. He was ready to battle and not in the mood for Lex's ill-timed humor.

"I believe it's possible, and the details are most likely recorded somewhere. But that information is useless without the daggers," Macie said.

Every time I grabbed onto a sliver of hope, it felt like someone stomped on my hand until I was forced to let go. "And you don't know where they might be?"

Macie shook her head. "My children searched for them for years and others before them, all unsuccessfully. But consider this. If you find the daggers, between those and the abilities the other spirits and I gifted you, the three of you could be the strongest siblings yet to face Cora."

Lex leaned forward and propped his elbows on his knees. "Okay. A lot of our relatives are still living in this house in spirit form, right?"

Macie nodded.

"Why can't you just ask if anyone knows where they are? At least one of them was responsible for hiding them. I mean, is there a ghost clubhouse where you all hang out and relive the good old days? Maybe a yearly family reunion or something like that?"

I stared at Lex in surprise. That had to be one of his better ideas. One in a sea of others ranging from brainless to death awaits you around the corner. But it was something.

Macie smiled. "I wish it was that easy, Lex. But no, we rarely run into each other. Where we are, there are many planes and times. Some spirits may see the house as it was when they were living. Others may not even be in the house, but somewhere on the grounds or wherever their lives ended. I'm able to be here with you because I felt a strong connection with this house and an obligation to warn you about the dangers that come with being a Teller."

Lex slumped back into the chair and exhaled. "Okay. Let's take a tally. We have a seriously pissed off ghost who bestowed a curse on our family, which up to this point has been one hundred percent effective. Three daggers, our only defense against her, went missing decades ago, and we have no clue where they could be. We're seriously screwed."

No one disagreed with his assessment. The future looked bleak from where we stood.

Lex rose from the chair, his gaze resting on each of us for a beat. "If life gives us lemons? I say we hurl them back with everything we've got."

CHAPTER TWELVE

Since Macie laid all the cards on the table and my brothers and I knew we fell under the curse umbrella, we'd been hyper-vigilant around the house. Just days ago, our home echoed with laughter and a sense of relief. The thunderhead of financial tensions hadn't entirely disappeared, but it had eased, and we finally had a permanent place to call home. But now? It was like a fragile glass dome covered the house and the slightest impact would shatter the carefully constructed façade.

Dad's first instinct was to pack us up and get as far away as possible. Macie said he wouldn't be the first Teller to try that option. Cora still found them, and the outcome was always the same. Death. Our best option was to search for the daggers and kill Cora or reunite her with Iona.

We kept waiting for Cora to appear around the next corner or for her to strike one of us dead as we slept or ate breakfast. Was a formal invitation to duel required? Maybe surprise attacks were more her style. She'd have to test us at some point to gauge our strength, we just didn't know when or how. From what Macie said, we knew it was important the three of us never be far from each other. We all had jobs, but with Mystic Harbor being a small town, each of us could be home within ten minutes. A lot could happen in ten minutes, but what more we could do at this point, I didn't know. Finding those daggers was crucial if we were to protect our family, end the curse, and send Cora to the hell she deserved after over a century of murdering Tellers.

I was on my way outside to paint the porch before heading to the bookstore this afternoon. As I passed Harper's room, I heard her talking to someone. That wasn't anything unusual. She spoke to her dolls, stuffed animals, imaginary friends. Harp just enjoyed talking. She and Lex shared that trait.

My brothers and I had attended many tea parties in our time, the three of us sitting at Harper's small, pink table while holding tiny, flowered cups. Harp insisted our pinkies stick out, saying it was the proper way to drink tea. Feathered boas were also required, and Harp had plenty to choose from. We obeyed since we were putty in her hands and did whatever she asked of us.

She also liked to play salon. At our prior school, Gid proudly sported pink and purple sparkly nail polish on alternating fingers for weeks until it eventually wore off. Some guys on his football team tried to kid him about it, but one growl from Gid stopped them cold. With both sides of Lex's head shaved, Harp had pulled the long hair on top into a ponytail. That wasn't unusual, but where Lex generally wore it high on the back of his head, Harp thought it looked better on the top of his head. It splayed out like water you'd see in a large fountain in the park. It was emerald green that week, so it was a pretty good likeness. She'd insisted my black-framed glasses hid my eyes, and I'd sat still for nearly an hour as she applied bright blue eyeshadow. Harp topped off my look with a rosy pink blush. Like I said, Harper held our hearts in her small hands.

But today something felt off to me, and instinct told me to stop and listen. The door was cracked about six inches, and I gently pushed it open wider to get a better view.

Her usual favorite stuffed animals—Loki, Rex, and Percy—were gathered around the table at what looked like a tea party. Pink and blue plates and cups sat before each guest. But there were five places set instead of four. Maybe an imaginary friend was also on the guest list. Wouldn't be the first time there was a guest only visible to her.

"I like living here," Harp said, as she poured tea for Loki the cat. "I have my own bedroom, and so do my brothers." She set the teapot down and turned to the empty space at the table as if she was listening to someone. "Maybe your little girl would like to play with me sometime. It's fun making new friends."

I felt a tightening in my chest. My gut urged me to rush in, grab Harper, and get her out of there. My more rational side said this could be purely innocent, and I didn't want to scare her for no reason.

Harper's face twisted in sadness. "Your little girl is lost? How long has it been since you've seen her?"

The cup at the empty space at the table rose into the air as if someone lifted it to their mouth. My breath caught as I reminded myself spirits filled this house, and Harp could be talking to a distant cousin for all I knew. We hadn't told her about our deceased family members roaming freely about the house, but Harper sure didn't seem alarmed to be speaking with a supernatural being at her tea party. I had to be certain.

I pushed the door open wider and watched the floating cup slowly lower to the table. I caught a vague shimmer in the seat as I approached my sister. "Who are you talking to, Harp?"

She twisted her mouth in disapproval as she glared at me. "You interrupted my party, Beck."

"I just wondered who your guests are. Loki, Rex, and Percy are old friends, but who's in that seat?" I asked, gesturing toward the empty one across from her.

"It's a lady who's lived here a long time and was lonely until we moved in. Cause the house was empty for so long."

Even as I stared at the seat, the shimmering grew more distinct. "Did you say she had a daughter?"

Harp nodded. "And she hasn't seen her for lots of years. She really misses her. Don't you think that's sad, Beck? Mom would miss us if we couldn't be together."

I moved closer to Harp, not taking my eyes off whoever occupied the chair. "She sure would. What's your friend's name?"

"Cora. Isn't that a pretty name?"

I lunged toward Harper and swung her into my arms as I yelled for my brothers. "Gid! Lex! In Harper's room now!" I'd heard Gid moving about in his room before I left my own, and since Lex's door was shut, I knew he hadn't left for work yet. He left his door open if he wasn't home. I only hoped Gid didn't have his headphones on.

Gid's door slammed against the wall as he threw it open, then his feet thundered down the hall toward us. He halted in the doorway and looked at us questioningly. "What's wrong?"

I gestured toward the chair. "Cora." As I spoke her name, her shape became more distinct since Gid was also in the room. Shimmering particles swirled like white dandelion puffs to form into the shape of a woman. Black, wavy hair flowed down her back, and her lips slid into a sinister smirk. Flat, soulless eyes gazed back at us.

Gid shouldered past us into the room and positioned himself between Cora and Harper and me, staring her down. "Get Harper out of here. Take her to Dad in the garage and get Lex. Hurry."

I didn't want to leave Gid alone with Cora, but Harper's safety came before anything else. I rushed out of the room as Harp demanded to know why we were taking her away from her friend. My stomach was in knots and my heart pounded as I sprinted down the stairs and outside to the garage where Dad had been repairing a bookshelf for most of the morning.

Harper still screamed her displeasure as I set her down. "Keep Harp here. Don't let her out of your sight." The panicked look on my face said it all, and Dad immediately scooped Harper up into his arms and closed the garage door behind me as I rushed back into the house and bounded upstairs. I silently prayed Gid would be okay.

My chest heaved as I threw open Lex's door. He was lying on his bed listening to music, headphones in place. He ripped them off his head and leaped off the bed to follow me, no questions asked.

We rushed into Harper's room two doors down the hallway.

"—out of here," Gid said as we entered the room.

Cora was invisible to Gid since I'd left the room, but she appeared when Lex and I entered. "And here are the other two. Finally, all three of you together. I've been waiting quite a while for this. Harper has told me so much about you." Her voice was coarse and gravelly with a thick Scottish accent.

"Don't even think of laying a finger on her," Lex said, his face stern. Usually the jokester, it was odd to see such a serious expression on him.

Cora tilted her head to the side and smiled. "She's quite delightful, really. Children are so innocent. She reminds me of my daughter."

Gid snorted. "You mean the daughter that killed her classmates? Harper isn't a murderer."

Cora's head whipped in Gid's direction, and she rested her fiery gaze on him. "Be careful what you say to me. Iona was just a child when she died. She didn't understand what happened to her."

Lex scoffed. "Sounds like the blame should have been on the parents. Guess you didn't do your job and teach her right from wrong."

Was he *trying* to get us killed sooner? This was the first time we'd encountered Cora, and we were unprepared. No daggers, no weapons of any kind, no talismans. Not that we'd have known the kind we needed. We didn't even have a leaf of sage for smudging. Maybe I could negotiate with her. Get her to see reason. Based on all the graves in the cemetery, that technique hadn't worked before, but it cost nothing to try again. I hoped, anyway.

"Look, we know you could kill us right now. What do you want? What can we do to make you leave our family alone?"

She considered each of us with her ominous black eyes. They sparkled with hatred over something we'd had no hand in. "Only one thing will cancel the curse. Bring my daughter back. Her soul splintered when your ancestors stabbed her. The shards were absorbed into the daggers so she can't even find peace. If I'm reunited with my daughter, the curse is over. If not, I'll continue my promise to end the Teller line." She smiled wickedly. "I'll even let you choose who will be first."

Cold gripped my heart. "My immediate family, our parents, my brothers and I, and especially Harper, never did anything to hurt you or your daughter. We shouldn't be held responsible for the actions of our ancestors."

"You'll pay for their sins!" Cora shouted, hurtling out of her chair. It flew across the room and struck the wall, where it shattered into pieces.

The three of us leaped back, and again I cursed the fact that we were so unprepared. How could we have known Harper's imaginary friend was Cora? How had we missed something so crucial?

Gid recovered first. "We don't know how to release your daughter from the daggers. Even if we did, we don't know where they're hidden."

Cora's voice returned to her original sickly sweet, teasing tone. "Then I suggest you figure it out. You're lucky I'd grown bored since Macie died. It was a long year alone in this house. Since you've been here, I've been having fun playing with the three of you for a while, giving you time to meet my demands. But the second you're of no use to me and stop trying to find the daggers... Well, you know what will happen. I suggest you get started. You wouldn't want my patience to wane again. You have two weeks." She disappeared from sight, but we heard her clearly, as if she were still standing in front of us. "Remember, the innocent Harper will take the place of the first one of you to fall."

With those words, pain sliced through my chest.

• • •

"Anyone have a brilliant psychotic ghost-killing plan they'd like to share?" Lex asked.

The three of us were gathered in Lex's room. Our first encounter with the vengeful spirit who'd killed a vast number of our family had shaken us to our cores. But we were also angry. Angry that none of us was responsible for what happened to Cora's daughter. Enraged that she'd threaten Harper, who'd never hurt anyone. Incensed that we were helpless, having nothing at our disposal to fight Cora with. How were we going to protect our family?

Gid paced about the room, muttering to himself. If he couldn't be physical, that was his technique for working through things. It was also a way to prevent himself from getting physical. None of us liked situations out of our control, but Gid especially had an aversion to an inability to protect his family and friends. He and Lex may go at it, and there had been times their tussles became a full-on Teller family brawl, but he'd also defend Lex with everything he had if someone outside our family threatened him. He met challenges head on, whereas Lex tried to joke his way out, and I rationalized and negotiated.

So far, none of these techniques had proved effective.

"We've got to find those daggers," I said. "We can't confront Cora again with nothing to defend ourselves."

Gid stopped pacing. "We need to learn about the talismans. The holy water and chains in the garage might also help." He picked up his path again between Lex's bed and the closet.

Lex threw himself down crossways on the bed, arms over his head. "Yeah, we were pretty easy target practice for her. But the daggers could be in the house or a million other places. Where would we even start looking?"

"If Macie knew who'd hidden them all those years ago, maybe we could attempt to contact their spirit and just ask," I suggested.

"Have you noticed the ghosts roaming this house are generally the same crowd? Oh, wait. You probably haven't since I'm the one who can see them. You'll have to take my word for it. Macie was right. Even though they're not at rest, the spirits exist on different planes. It's not like we can put out wanted signs with a picture asking if someone has seen a certain ghost." He frowned. "Wait, we can't do that, can we?"

Gid stopped pacing again and turned to face us. "If ghosts exist on different planes, is it possible for us to go where they are? We've seen movies where people have out-of-body experiences, right? Maybe there's a hidden door somewhere to take us to one of those planes."

Lex propped himself up on an elbow. "Normally I'd tell you how stupid that idea sounds. But normally we don't live in a house filled with ghosts who hold conversations with us. So maybe a hidden door to another plane is a thing. This sounds like a Macie question to me."

I leaned against the desk and started chewing on my thumbnail. It was an old habit and something I used to do when stressed. I pulled it back out, refusing to reactivate bad habits. If traveling to another plane was even possible, maybe I could study the family history books and narrow down which generation was the last to use the daggers. Macie and her sons might have overlooked something that could help us. It was worth a try.

Traveling to another spirit plane. If someone had told me a month ago this would be my life, I'd have sooner believed the sky was purple. I had some research to do.

• • •

I'd just locked the front door behind the last customer of the day when Everline called to me from her office. "Beck, can I see you before you leave for the night?"

"Of course." Had I done something wrong? I mentally ran through everything I'd done on the job over the last few days, but nothing came to mind aside from the time Gid caused me to be late, and it had only happened once. Puzzled, I walked through the aisles, pausing to scratch Mr. Darcy under his chin. After entering Everline's office, I sat down across from her.

"Have I done something wrong?"

"Of course not. It's nothing like that."

Well, that was a relief. I loved working around books, but I also loved working for Everline. She was the best boss I'd had, and I'd hate to lose this job.

"Beck, you know I think highly of you. You're a good employee. Your head's on straight, which I can't always say for people your age. You're an intelligent young man. I'm glad you and Willow are friends. No one can ever have too many."

I sensed a "but" coming. I hadn't told Everline about the curse, but she seemed to have a good sense of it from her conversations with Macie.

"But from what I've seen when the two of you are around each other, I'm getting the feeling both of you would like your friendship to be more."

Blood creeped up from my neck all the way to the roots of my hair. Was I in trouble for crushing on my boss's granddaughter? "Well, um..."

Everline waved her hand in the air. "No need to be embarrassed now. I've raised Willow since she was five." When my brows furrowed, she gave a sad smile. "Her parents were killed in a car accident. I may be biased, but between her parents' influence and my own, she's grown into beautiful, kind, intelligent young woman. You'd be crazy not to take notice of her in my opinion." She leaned forward and propped her elbows on the desk, hands clasped beneath her chin. "What worries me is what's going on at your house. I've known for quite a while that things aren't exactly normal there. Too many deaths. The feelings I'd get while visiting Macie.

Some of the stories she told were the stuff of nightmares. I even remember her mumbling something about a curse, but when I asked her about it, she said I must have misheard what she said. Then there's the paranormal business and Macie's ghost still lingering around the house."

My stomach dropped and took my heart along with it. I knew what was coming. The situation at our house was precarious, and we had no way of knowing what would happen next, let alone the outcome. And she had an inkling of the curse. Macie might have denied it, but Everline was smart enough to know there was something to it. With this curse, I could be dead tomorrow, next week, or next year. Worse, people around us—innocent, unrelated people like Willow—could be caught in the crossfire. Until we located those daggers, my brothers and I were on borrowed time, and so was anyone in our orbit.

Everline sighed deeply, but her voice was full of concern. "What I'm trying to say, Beck, is that I don't want Willow to be put in danger. Seeing her here in the store is fine. So are the beach and restaurants, and wherever else she and her friends go. But I don't want her anywhere near your house."

"No, ma'am." I shook my head. "I'd never put Willow in danger, or anyone else outside our family. It's bad enough that our own safety is uncertain. I'd never want to drag innocent people into this mess."

I must have looked like a puppy kicked to the curb because Everline rose from her chair, walked around the desk, and squatted in front of me. She placed her hand over mine, and her face was full of pity. "Oh, honey. Your family should never have been put in this situation. Lord knows Macie tried to keep you out of it. More than anything, I want you to be free of whatever's hanging over your house, Beck. You should be enjoying this summer before your senior year, making new friends, and going on dates with Willow—if that's what you both want.

"But because of your last name, you drew the short straw in life. I have faith you'll get through this, and I'll do anything I can to help. I know that's not much, but having people on your side is better than being alone."

How right Everline was. Only Gid, Lex, and I could fight Cora, we knew that. No one else could help us. Knowing we had a support system made it just a little better and edged up the confidence level. At least I could talk to Everline about some of the madness in my life right now.

But she wouldn't need to worry about Willow. I'd never bring her to the house.

CHAPTER THIRTEEN

The roiling cloud of a death curse still hung over our heads, but daily life moved on. Traveling to an undead plane was the only idea we'd come up with, but the name of the relative who'd last handled the daggers needed to be researched so we knew who to look for once we got there. I'd started looking, and Gid picked up where I'd left off. He was in the library studying the history books right now. There was also the little detail about how exactly one crossed over and remained living. We hadn't found that hidden door, and somehow I expected it to be more difficult than that.

Life continued because we didn't want to scare Harper or pique her curiosity any more than necessary, especially after the incident with Cora, so we needed to pretend everything was normal. Or as close to it as possible.

After Cora departed the very memorable tea party, we'd sat down with Harper to talk about what happened. She seemed to think we were finally able to see her invisible friends, which sounded like a logical explanation to her. None of us wanted to correct her impression. Telling her who Cora really was would only upset her, so we'd explained that Cora wasn't someone she should speak to, no matter how nice she seemed. If Harper saw her again, she was to tell one of us immediately. Stubbornness was one of her stronger personality traits, so she'd argued and complained but eventually quit bickering and seemed to grasp the seriousness of the situation.

This morning, I was back to chores. Painting was probably my least favorite thing on Dad's list. I didn't mind yard work or minor repairs, but I'd been the last to wake up and got stuck with the leftovers. Gid and Lex hated it as much as I did. Now, the temperature over ninety degrees, the summer sun beating down from overhead, I was stuck painting the outside walls of the garage. My T-shirt and shorts and probably my hair sported the same charcoal gray color as the walls. Just another reason I hated painting.

Something about the conversation with Harper about Cora and her other invisible friends bothered me. I felt like I'd missed something. Harper hadn't thought it was strange that she could see Cora. She'd seen imaginary friends for years. But Cora obviously wasn't imaginary. Not to us.

Then I dropped the paintbrush and silently cursed myself at being so oblivious.

What if all of Harper's imaginary friends weren't really imaginary? What if they were spirits like Cora? Had Harp been seeing ghosts all this time?

I stood there in shock, turning over ideas, until Lex rounded the corner of the garage. He flopped down on the grass in a shady spot, then stretched his legs in front of him and leaned back on his hands. A welcome breeze lifted damp hair off the back of my neck, but unfortunately it blew the smell of his sweat in my direction.

I wrinkled my nose in disgust.

"You know Dad said to paint the garage and not the grass, right?"

I borrowed one of Gid's moves and flipped him off before bending over and picking up the brush off the ground. It was covered in grass and dirt, so I'd need to get a fresh one from the garage.

"Remember when I mentioned the number of dead relatives parading around our house had decreased?"

"Sure." I wiped my paint covered hand on my shorts.

He'd mentioned it a few days ago, but I'd been neck deep in the family history books and hadn't thought much about it. My epiphany about Harp's imaginary friends was something I'd have to think about before I discussed it with anyone. I slid it to the backburner.

"We're missing more. It's not like they held gatherings in rooms or had game nights, but I'd see random people pass through regularly. Most of them didn't even stop to say hi. Rude." He paused a beat. "Something's changed, Beck."

I turned to look at him. It was a rare occasion when Lex sounded serious about anything, but when he did, I paid attention. This was one of those occasions. "Any idea what's going on?"

He shrugged. "This is all uncharted territory for me. I mentioned it to Gid, and chatter around the house has quieted down. He's been catching more Zs at night."

I ran my hand through my hair. Which was a stupid thing to do since it was covered in paint. "Cora's prevented them from crossing, so where could they go? It's not like ghosts can just cross over on their own, right? They'd have done it years ago if it was possible."

A faint giggle came from the direction of the hydrangea bush a few yards behind Lex. It was a very familiar giggle, and I knew exactly who it belonged to. I looked at my younger brother.

I held a finger to my lips to silence him. He nodded and started talking about his surfing lesson earlier this week. While he described his daring adventure in a wave tunnel, which absolutely never happened, I circled around and came up behind Harp, where she'd crouched behind the bush. Loki, Rex, and Percy sat beside her on the grass.

"Gotcha!" I picked Harper up and swung her into the air as she squealed in delight. Her laugh was one of the best sounds in the world, and I'd never tire of it. Gid rushed around the side of the house, a murderous expression on his face. He must have finished his research shift and thought Harper was in trouble. Gid relaxed when he saw she was safe.

Lex walked back to Harper's hiding place. "Listening again when you're not supposed to, Harp? You know what Mom said about that."

I put Harp down. She spun around to face Lex, hands on her hips. "I was here first playing. Not my fault you two started talking."

"Did you hear what we were saying?" I asked.

Harp sat down on the grass again, picked up Rex, and brushed dirt off his back. "You were talking about the dead people that used to live here."

Gid's mouth dropped open as he gaped at us. "Seriously? You two idiots talked about that with her only fifteen feet away?"

Harp glared at Gid in disapproval. "Not supposed to say that word, Gid."

Lex ignored his comment. He raised his eyebrows as he met my gaze over Harper's head, then looked down at her again. "What do you know about dead people that used to live here?"

"I met a lot of them the day we moved in. They're nice. Some of them told me stories about when they lived in our house."

I lowered myself to the grass in front of Harper while Lex and Gid kneeled on either side of her.

"You can see and talk to the people who used to live here?" Gid asked.

She nodded.

"And you're not scared?"

Harp's eyes widened. "Why would I be scared? They're just family we never met, and they're fun to play with. This used to be their home, and then they died. They were supposed to leave but couldn't. So, I help them."

Lex covered his mouth in shock. This was the first time I'd ever seen him speechless. Gid looked like he was wrestling with the decision to hear Harper out or swoop her up and carry her far away from here. Not only was Harper unafraid of ghosts, she'd also been communicating with them longer than the three of us. Even more shocking was while it took Lex, Gid, and me together to manifest the spirits and talk to them, Harper had done it on her own.

"How do you help them, Harp?" I asked gently.

Harper continued playing, making Loki the cat tackle Percy the rabbit. "I bring the light."

"What kind of light?" Gid's voice was anxious, and I knew Harper would pick up on it.

"The light, silly. The one that lets them leave."

Lex swallowed hard, then picked up Rex the dinosaur and held him close, almost as if he needed comforting. "Where do they go?"

Harper looked at us as if we were stupid, then rolled her eyes. "They go to the good place where they can see the people they love and be happy. For big brothers, you're not very smart sometimes."

"They go to the good place," Lex whispered, still in disbelief.

I pointed toward the garage. "The three of us have to talk about something that's private, Harp. You remember what private means, right?"

"Course I do. I can remember lots of things." She turned back to her stuffed animals.

Lex sat Rex gently back down on the ground, seeming reluctant to part with him, then we stood and headed over to the far side of the garage where Harp couldn't hear us. As we walked away from her, she called out in a singsong voice, "But I know you're talking about me!"

"She's..." Gid started.

"Yeah," I said.

"Wow." Lex shook his head in wonder. "That's why ghost traffic slacked off. She's helping them cross over. How is that possible?"

"It takes the three of us together to communicate with the spirits, and each of us brings something to the process. Harp does it all on her own. Macie said the spirits gave us abilities. Maybe crossing over is Harper's," Gid said.

"That doesn't make sense." I shook my head. "If the spirits had that ability, they'd have used it themselves."

Then an incredible realization dawned on me. Harp's imaginary friends and my earlier epiphany. What Harp just said changed everything. She'd seen spirits for years. The odds were slim that all our previous homes were haunted, but maybe ghosts were drawn to her. They sensed she could help them. That had to be it.

"Okay. You might think I'm crazy, but consider this," I said. "Remember all Harp's imaginary friends? What if they were spirits? Spirits that sought her out and asked for her help to cross the veil?"

Lex's eyes widened as he dropped to the ground again almost as if his legs wouldn't support him. He stared into space, catatonic at this point.

Gid fell back against the garage wall and leaned over with his hands on his knees, silent for a long moment. Then he stood again and ran his hands over his face. "If that's true, she's seen ghosts all this time and was never scared. What a brave kid. And what a gift."

Lex finally came to his senses. "Don't you people realize what this means?" Gid and I stared at him and waited, knowing Lex would answer the question himself. "We've been living in haunted houses and apartments with ghosts hanging out like they were part of the family. We even dined with them! Remember how Mom had to set places at the table? They sat there and watched us eat." A look of horror crept over his face. "And maybe watched us sleep. They could have been sitting right there on the side of the bed staring at us, sucking out our souls!"

Gid rolled his eyes. "Would you stop? They're not Dementors, Lex. Our souls are all intact."

"Do I really need to remind you that you were the one who thought it would be cool to meet a ghost?" I asked. "Let's stay on track. I don't like leaving Harp by herself for too long."

Lex flipped me off—we were a family of loving gestures—then waved his hand in the air as if saying to continue.

Gid turned to me. "Part of Cora's curse is not letting these spirits rest in peace, and she's been keeping them here for decades. Why doesn't she know about this?"

I pushed my glasses up. "Harp's gift must be powerful. If Cora finds out, she'll be furious."

"How could she not know? Seems like she'd take a head count regularly, don't you think?" Lex still clung to the idea of our deceased relatives meeting at a local clubhouse where Cora took roll.

"Remember what Macie said about the spirits moving on different planes," I reminded him. "Maybe Cora can't travel to all of them. Or she's gotten accustomed to them being here and quit paying attention. No one's been able to help them for over a century, so why should anything be different now?"

"Harp doesn't understand why our relatives are trapped here. What if Cora takes her anger out on our sister?" Lex's eyes filled with fear.

Anger and worry rolled off Gid. He always looked for the quickest solution to problems, and we were about as far from that as possible. "Maybe Mom and Dad should take her and leave. Get her somewhere safe."

I shook my head. "We already talked about this. If that was possible, we'd have left weeks ago. Cora can follow us, remember? She latched onto Klaus back in Scotland and traveled from one continent to another. Moving from city to city or state to state would be child's play to her. It doesn't matter where we go. She'll find us."

Everywhere we turned, a barrier blocked our path. We just needed one break. Maybe then a solution would be unlocked. Anything to give us the advantage we desperately needed. And then a light bulb lit brightly in my brain.

"Remember how we talked about venturing to a new plane to search for the spirit who hid the daggers? Or finding anyone who could tell us where they were? What if Harper can open that door for us?"

"No. No way." Gid crossed his arms. "You can shut down that idea right now. We're not putting Harp in danger."

"But she's been doing it all along," Lex said. "The spirit club numbers are down, and all the jabber you hear has quieted. Harp's fine. If it looked like she was in any danger, we'd immediately stop."

"Come on, Gid, you know we'd never put Harp at risk. Anyone that threatened her would have to get through all of us first. But why don't we question her some more about the light?" I suggested. "Maybe she's seen other doorways but doesn't know what they are."

Gid still didn't look convinced, but he gave a slight nod of his head. At least he was willing to try.

We left the privacy of the garage and returned to Harper. It looked like we'd interrupted a safari. She, Rex, Loki, and Percy hid behind another hydrangea bush and watched a bird in the grass several yards away.

"Harp, we wanted to ask you more about the light," I said. "Is that okay?"

She continued inching her animals toward the unsuspecting bird, completely unaware of the gravity of the information she'd dropped on us. Like kids spoke to ghosts every day and it was a natural occurrence. "Sure. What do you want to know?"

"How do you make the light appear?"

"When the people come to me, I close my eyes and think hard about helping them. When I open my eyes, the light is there waiting for them. It makes them happy. Sometimes they even cry, but they're not sad tears. Then they thank me and walk through."

"That's nice of you, Harp," Lex said.

"Some have been waiting a really long time to leave here," Harper added. "I like helping them."

"Remember when we lived at other places, and you had imaginary friends?" I asked. Harper focused on her animals again but nodded. "Were those friends like the people here?"

"Yep," Harp said, popping the p.

"What did they want?" Gid asked.

"Sometimes they just wanted to talk because they didn't have any friends. Some wanted to leave through the door and go to the good place. Some of them didn't want anything. They just liked being around our family because we made them happy."

I was in awe of my little sister. At such a young age, she'd communicated with ghosts and thought of them as friends. Maybe she'd even seen them as a toddler and thought they were part of the family. She wasn't afraid of them and accepted this was a normal situation.

"Why didn't you tell anyone about the ghosts?" I asked.

"I did. Mom and Dad called them imaginary friends, so that's what I thought they were," she said matter-of-factly. All this time she'd been telling us what she'd seen, and no one believed her. The people who loved her most chalked it up to make believe, a child's overactive imagination. I resolved right then and there to always listen to Harp and never make assumptions.

"Harp, the people here, where do they come from? The ones that need help?" I asked.

Her brows furrowed, and she looked at me like I was stupid. "From inside the house. Duh."

Gid and Lex didn't even try to hide their snickering.

"But do you know exactly where in the house? Are there different places?"

"Course. They use doors. Not like the ones in our bedrooms. Sometimes I can't see them. But sometimes I can. The ghosts open them and come into our house."

"Have you ever tried to go through those doors?" Lex asked.

She shook her head. "They said I'm not supposed to. I could get lost and not be able to find my way back. Mom and Dad wouldn't know where to find me."

"That's right, Harp," Gid said. "You need to always remember that. Don't ever try to follow them through those doors, okay? You stay on this side with us."

She nodded. The bird flew away, and I could tell Harp was getting bored with this conversation. She wanted to move on to something else. "Can I ask you one more question?"

She sighed in exasperation and rolled her eyes.

I almost told her they'd get stuck like that, and then couldn't believe I'd nearly channeled Mom.

"Just one more. I want to go play."

"Could you show us where those doors are?"

"Course. There's one in your bedroom." She picked up her stuffed animals and skipped toward the house.

Now I was the speechless one. These spirits were my family and weren't harmful. I knew that. But the thought of them entering and exiting a doorway to different planes just feet from where I slept nearly paralyzed me. What Lex said earlier about them sucking out our souls put images in my head I had to blink hard to suppress.

I decided I could live with a spirit doorway in my room because at least we had something to work with now. It might be the advantage we needed.

CHAPTER FOURTEEN

Turns out I couldn't live with a spirit door in my room. Our family took up five bedrooms, but there were still others in the house that stood vacant. Previous Tellers had room for more than one generation to live here at a time. With that freaky doorway in my room, I planned on sleeping in another bedroom. Several options were available.

My parents' bedroom was on the first floor, but the four of us were on the second floor. I wanted to keep it that way and stay close to my siblings in case there was another incident with Cora. We'd taken the four rooms closest to each other, but there were two more rooms at the end of the hall that were unused and unexplored. The third floor also had rooms, but I hadn't checked out that area yet. The thought of how much space we had still boggled my mind.

Opening the door to the first one on our floor, I found an average bedroom furnished with a queen size bed, chest of drawers, and bookshelf. Several family photos sat atop the chest and bookshelf. The window overlooked the backyard, where I heard Harper giggling as she played hide and seek with Gid and Lex. It was never challenging to find her. She always hid in the same spot her opponent just abandoned the previous round. We pretended we didn't notice.

This room would do, but I still had one more to check out. The second I stepped into the last bedroom, a feeling of sorrow settled over me. It was heavy and oppressive, and I'd never felt anything like it. This room was smaller than the others. A twin bed with a pale pink quilt atop it stood in the middle of the room, and a wooden chest sat on the floor at the foot of it. Lying on the pillow was a doll with long brown hair and a light blue dress. The only other furniture in the room was a small dresser. A yellowed teddy bear that was probably once white leaned against a ballerina doll on the floor beside the dresser.

I stepped over to the closet, careful not to disturb anything. Not that anyone would know, but it just felt wrong somehow. Like I was intruding in someone's private space. Various types of clothing sized for a young girl hung neatly inside the closet, along with more toys in a basket on the floor.

This had been a child's room someone had lovingly preserved as if she was still here. It could have belonged to any number of Tellers, but I had a feeling this room had been Emily's, Macie's daughter. I remembered her headstone in the cemetery listed her as ten years old when she'd died, and my heart ached all over again for Macie. She'd suffered so many losses in her life but tried to help us even in death. First with the year delay in locating us, and now as a ghost.

Staying in this bedroom wasn't a possibility. It didn't belong to me, and I'd never take it from Emily. Maybe she still visited here from time to time.

I'd slept in the first room I'd checked out that overlooked the back yard. Well, I'd actually stared at the ceiling for hours before giving up and reading. Thinking about the spirits walking freely about my bedroom kind of freaked me out a little. Changing my bedroom permanently was rapidly becoming a distinct possibility.

Telling Mom and Dad about our plan wasn't an option. They'd try to stop us, so that's why we'd waited until they left with Harper to run errands. We'd drawn straws to see who'd go through the doorway. I'd never noticed it in my bedroom before, but when Gid,

Lex, and I went into the room intending to locate it, there it was in all its glory. The door was barely noticeable in the corner, opposite my bed. It was easy to miss unless you knew what you were looking for. It caused a faint shimmer in the air, like an oily rainbow in a water puddle when the light hit it just right. If you stared at the doorway straight on, you'd notice something off. Like things didn't seem to line up correctly.

Getting back to the straw situation, I'd lost. Or won depending on how you looked at it. I was going through the doorway. Because of Poltergeist, an eighties movie we'd watched with our parents years ago, tying a rope around my waist seemed like a good idea. At least it made me feel a little safer. We weren't sure who or what I'd encounter on the other side, but I focused on the fact that my relatives were across the threshold and meant no harm. Our goal was to help all the Tellers.

Gid and Lex would stay on this side and hang onto the rope. I put my complete faith and trust in them to pull me out if something happened. But I'd also threatened them about getting distracted by some petty disagreement. An altercation between them might result in my rope being dropped, and then it could be bye-bye Beck permanently.

The thought crossed my mind that I might see nothing. I amplified Gid's and Lex's abilities. We'd gotten stronger, but maybe it would take all three of us to communicate, even through the veil. Then who would stay on this side to pull us back through if something happened? We faced so many uncertainties, but the only way to find out was to try.

I checked the rope around my waist once more and tightened it again. "Do you need me to push you through?" Lex asked. "I'm only offering because you know I like to help out where I can."

I threw him a cutting glare. "Your job is to hang onto the rope. I'll get myself through the door." Okay, maybe I was procrastinating a little, but I didn't see either of my brothers volunteering to take my place. This was an inaugural trip, and we didn't know what would come of it.

Inhaling deeply, I turned toward the faint shimmer, then stopped and glanced over my shoulder one last time at Gid and Lex. "We've got you," Gid said. Lex nodded once in agreement.

"You'd better." Then I faced the doorway and stepped through.

●　　●　　●

Bright rays of midday sun had filled my bedroom, and I blinked hard as my eyes adjusted to the change in environment. Bright didn't describe this place at all. Vast differences existed between our world and theirs.

A rainbow of colors was absent. Only varying shades of gray, black, and white surrounded me. Filmy silhouettes that I assumed were people moved about me—or they used to be people. Their shapes wavered and morphed, their margins ill-defined. I made out an arm, then it blended in again with the spirit's trunk. A mouth appeared then dissolved. I wondered if my own features remained intact.

I also felt lighter than I did in our world. Not that I could float or anything. I just didn't seem to be the same weight. I lifted my arm, and the feeling was so foreign my limb could have belonged to another person.

Even though the shapes were blurry, I identified several spirits. Some moved independently of anyone. Others gathered in groups of two or more, almost as if they were communicating. Maybe they were. Maybe they were talking about us and how we could help them. Or how they could help us. Our situation was rocky. If we failed, the curse continued.

Some spirits ignored me and continued in their groups. Others wandered away. But a few seemed curious enough to break off from their circle and move toward me. It was clear I was an outsider in their world.

Being that I didn't fully understand this plane or how those who lived here would react to me, my first instinct was to run. Instead, I thought about how desperately we needed to find the daggers. How we were all in danger. How none of us could bear it if something happened to Harper. I forced my body to still and focused on why I was here.

Four shapes gathered around me. It was difficult to determine if they were male or female, but they were the size of adults.

In studying the family history diaries, we'd determined the last people to use the daggers were William, Mary, and Joseph Teller back in the early 1900s. As far as we could tell, anyway. The weapons had been missing for over a century. Cora had terrorized my family for over one hundred years. So many deaths. The weight of that felt oppressive. Stakes were incredibly high.

Then a thought struck me. With Harper's help, several spirits had already crossed over. What if William, Mary, and Joseph were included in those numbers? If that was the case, the daggers could be lost forever. Cue a roiling pit of despair in my stomach. I reminded myself it was just as likely they were stranded here with the other spirits, and there was no need to get ahead of myself. I breathed in deeply then exhaled slowly.

I suddenly realized I hadn't heard a sound since crossing over. My ears felt a dull pressure, like I needed to pop them. Would my voice even be audible? There was only one way to find out.

"My name is Beck Teller," I said to the four spirits gathered around me. My words sounded muffled, but that solved the question of them being heard. I hoped they heard me, too. "I'm looking for William, Mary, or Joseph Teller. Could you help me? Do you know if they're here?"

Since Macie had mentioned the presence of several planes, the odds of them being in this one were minimal, but maybe we'd get lucky. We sure could use a miracle.

"Can you speak?" No response, but they didn't leave. Macie was fully corporeal and able to communicate on our side, but there had only been a handful of others like her that we'd come across in the house. None of them carried on conversations to the same extent as Macie. Just the occasional random one word greeting. Spirits could have distinct personalities, just like people. If they were shy or outgoing when they were alive, that trait probably carried over when they passed. Of the four gathered around me, their shapes shifted in a constant state of motion, but they didn't utter a sound.

"William, Mary, or Joseph Teller," I repeated. "My family needs to find them. They could have information that would help us fight Cora." At the mention of Cora's name, the demeanor of the surrounding spirits changed from curious, bordering on friendly, to wildly frantic. The four of them skittered away from me, all headed in different directions. Those spirits who'd hung around but kept their distance quickly dispersed. It was chaos, almost as if a bomb had gone off. My shoulders slumped in disappointment as I watched them leave, taking any chance of finding the siblings with them.

But not everyone was gone. Another spirit, small enough to be a child, remained. He or she was bigger than Harper, maybe a few years older. It was difficult to tell with their filmy figures. It saddened me that someone so young had their life cut short.

"Can you help me?" I asked again.

The indistinct features gradually took on the shape of the face of a young girl with large, dark eyes and light hair that hung past her shoulders. She wore a long, white dress that resembled a nightgown, clutched a doll in her arms, and was nearly as solid as Macie.

"Leave," she whispered urgently. "She's coming." Immediately after her warning, the young girl's body slowly dissipated into a long wisp of grayish smoke that floated away from me.

I was alone.

Vibrations thundered beneath my feet and climbed up my legs. The hair on my head rose as if the air was electrified. All the spirits had fled, abandoning me. But something approached. My gut clenched, and I knew with deep certainty I needed to high tail it out of here immediately.

I spun toward the door I'd come through. Just as I took a step in that direction, my body was jerked away from it and hurled several feet through the air in the other direction. I grunted in pain as I landed hard on my shoulder, then quickly rolled to face whatever, or whomever, had attacked me.

Cora.

She was massive compared to the other spirits I'd seen and towered above me. Her hair writhed in coils around her head, similar to Medusa's snakes, and the glare on her face was murderous as she glowered at me.

"What have you done?" she screamed, her shrieks echoing all around me, even inside my brain.

I clutched my head and tried to answer her, but fear dried my mouth, and my voice refused to cooperate. If I was able to utter a sound, it would probably be a scream. She moved closer to me, and I struggled to get to my feet, commanding my limbs to obey. I couldn't defend myself lying down. My eyes searched wildly for the door, but everything around me was gray, and I'd become disoriented when Cora jerked me away from it.

"How did you get here?"

The rope. It would lead me in the direction of the doorway. Even if Cora followed me, maybe my brothers and I together could fight her off. I reached for it around my waist.

The rope was gone.

It must have come untied during the attack. Falling back to my hands and knees, I hurriedly searched for it in the mist that creeped in with Cora's arrival. If I couldn't locate the rope, there was no way I'd find my way back to the doorway. My heart hammered against my chest at the thought of being trapped here indefinitely. Terror stole the breath from my lungs.

I was untethered. And alone. With Cora.

"I've prevented the Teller family from finding peace after their deaths, trapping them in this realm for over a century. Watching them continue to linger year after year in misery brought me happiness. Until now. Some of them are gone." She leaned over, her rotting face only inches from my own, her fetid breath moist on my clammy skin. "How did you do it?"

Icy fingers of paralyzing fear spread through every inch of my body. I wanted to close my eyes and pretend I was anywhere but here. That this was just a horribly vivid nightmare, and I was safe in my bed and would wake up any second.

And then I remembered the look of joy on Harper's face as I tossed her into the air after I snuck up on her behind the hydrangea bush. How she had the ability to persuade her brothers to do anything and held our hearts in her tiny hands. She was the reason I needed to fight. Macie said if one of us fell, Harper would be the replacement. She didn't have a choice. I refused to be the person who put her in that position.

"Tell me!" she screamed.

I clenched my jaw and forced myself to meet Cora's soulless black eyes. "We helped them move on to where they should have gone after death. They've found peace." Cora studied my face so intently I wondered if she could peer inside my mind to see exactly how we'd done it. But it wasn't me, Gid, or Lex. It was Harper. And that was information I'd never give up, no matter what.

She roared in anger, the sound deafening. I took that opportunity to stumble away from her, covering my ears to protect them. If I'd thought the floor had vibrated earlier, it was nothing compared to the rumbling quakes now. My bones rattled, and I feared the ground would split beneath me.

Cora glared, hatred etched in her ghoulish features. "You dare to interfere with my curse? You *helped* them?"

My whole body trembled in fear, but I managed to nod.

"Your life was already mine to end. As punishment for your actions, I claim it today. Now. And that means your sweet little sister takes your place."

Cora lunged toward me, her outstretched hands resembling malformed claws. I ran blindly, my sense of direction completely screwed up, the rope lost somewhere in the mist. I imagined Cora was only inches away, her icy breath on my neck, but I was terrified to risk a look behind me. My stomach sank at the thought of my brothers being left alone to find the daggers. The thought of Harper taking my place nearly paralyzed me. My parents would bury an empty coffin since my body would never be found in this plane.

I vowed to fight until my last breath. Cora had to catch me first. Years of running ensured my stamina would hold out for miles. I chanced a glance behind me. She was close, but not as close as I'd expected. Since she'd dragged out this curse for so many years, it was evident she relished the thrill of the chase.

My heart pounded from fear and physical exertion, but I'd continue on until she killed me or I collapsed.

And then someone tackled me hard from the side, and we fell to the ground in a tangle of limbs.

"Get off me!" I yelled, punching blindly at Cora.

"Beck, stop! We have to get out right now!" Gid grasped my hand and hauled me to my feet.

Gid. Not Cora. My brother came for me.

My gaze darted to another rope wrapped around his waist. It led in the direction of the doorway into my room.

"Run!" he screamed, shoving me in front of him.

Cora roared in frustration behind us, but I didn't dare turn around. I'd been closer to the doorway than I'd thought. In the mist of gray and white, a faint shimmer caught my eye about fifty feet away. I wanted to chance a glance at Gid to make sure he was still with me, but before I could turn around, he called out. "I'm right behind you. Just run!"

The doorway was only feet away now. When I reached it, I dove through and crashed into Lex on the other side. Gid landed on top of me. The three of us tangled in a heap, arms and legs sticking out in every direction. I wasn't sure which were mine, but I was safe.

But was I?

"Is she still coming?" Cora could shoot through the door at any second, couldn't she? According to Harper, other spirits freely crossed the threshold whenever they wished, so it reasoned Cora must be able to do the same.

"Hurry and check the salt line," Gid said.

"On it." Lex had already disentangled himself and was pouring another line over the top of the first. Would it work? We watched anxiously, waiting for her to burst through the doorway. Seconds became minutes. Either the salt had worked or she'd retreated momentarily to return another time. I knew she wasn't gone for good.

I rolled onto my back and ran my hands through my hair, chest heaving as I tried to catch my breath. I was still alive. If Gid hadn't come for me, there's no doubt in my mind Harper would be the third sibling required to battle Cora. "How did you know?" I asked. "How did you know I was in trouble?"

Gid stood and began untying the rope from his waist. "We felt a big jerk and then the rope went slack. Lex and I pulled it back, but you weren't there. We did rock, paper, scissors and I lost, so I had to go through the doorway and look for you."

A half-hearted laugh slipped out at Gid's attempt at a joke. "You lost?"

"No, idiot." He rolled his eyes. "I picked up the rope, tied it to me, then jumped through the doorway. Lex lashed the other end to your bed just in case."

Lex set the box of salt on my desk. "You really think we'd leave you there? I mean, I'm not saying the thought didn't cross my mind. One less brother to deal with and all that."

This was our way. We'd always handled tough situations with humor. Maybe it was just a guy thing, but it worked for us. I knew they loved me as I loved them. We just tended to stamp down those emotions deep, deep inside. My brothers always had my back, and I had theirs. We'd need each other more than ever if we were going to win this thing. But I'd also noticed the quiver in Lex's voice and the wobble in Gid's step.

Then I remembered.

"She knows," I said.

Gid and Lex looked at me in confusion.

"About some of the spirits crossing over."

Their looks of confusion turned to terror.

I shook my head. "She doesn't know it's Harper. Not yet, anyway."

But it was only a matter of time. Cora would come for all of us. Including Harp. We needed those daggers now more than ever.

CHAPTER FIFTEEN

"Beck! I need your help!" Mom screamed frantically from downstairs as I opened my bedroom door. She sounded scared.

"Daddy, you're hurt," Harper shrieked, then started crying.

I bolted down the stairs two at a time and jumped over the banister to the foyer ten steps from the bottom. My adrenaline spiked through the roof as I imagined the scenarios I might be running into. Was it Cora? How badly was Dad hurt? Was he even alive? Was anyone else hurt?

Mom called out instructions to Lex, and I heard the back door slam. I followed the sound of their voices into the kitchen and burst through the doorway into a bloody nightmare.

Water gushed full blast from the sink faucet. Blood-soaked dish towels lay on the floor, the counter, and the kitchen table where Dad sat in a chair. Sat wasn't the right word. He looked closer to toppling out of it.

"Harper, it's okay. I'll be fine." Dad tried to reassure Harp with a soothing tone, but pain clenched his voice.

Mom stood over him and wrapped another towel around a gushing wound in his right forearm. Harper sat on the floor sobbing. I rushed over and picked her up, then she wrapped her arms tightly around my neck and continued crying.

"I have to drive your dad to the emergency room. Stay with Harper. I'll call you when I know something," Mom said calmly as she held pressure on Dad's wound. His face was ashen, and the blood kept coming. Mom moved with purpose and efficiency. This wasn't her first rodeo with accidents. My brothers and I had seen the inside of emergency rooms more than once.

Lex burst through the back door and into the kitchen carrying duct tape. He pulled out a long strip and cut it, then wrapped it around the towel over Dad's wound as Mom held it in place.

"I'll drive," Lex said. "You sit in the back with Dad."

Mom grabbed her purse and car keys off the desk in the corner and moved toward the door. Dad's eyes rolled back in his head as he lost consciousness, and he tilted sideways in the direction of the floor.

"Lex!" I yelled, but he'd already noticed. He caught Dad before he fell, then picked him up in his arms and carried him out the back door.

"We'll call you," Mom said then slammed the door behind her.

• • •

Harper continued to sob against my shoulder. She was so scared. I needed to get her out of the kitchen and away from all the blood.

"Let's get you cleaned up, Harp." The closest bathroom on this floor was the ensuite in our parents' room. I carried her in there and sat her on the counter. My shirt was soaked from her tears and probably a lot of snot, but that was the least of my worries right now. She'd stopped crying for the moment, but her breath hitched every time she inhaled.

I wet a washcloth and wiped her face. "Hold out your hands." Small patches of blood dotted her hands and forearms, and I gently washed them off. "I know that was scary for you seeing Dad hurt. Do you want to talk about it?"

She nodded. Her glistening gray eyes were red-rimmed and full of confusion and fear. Harp was trying to be so brave, and my heart broke for her. "Will Daddy be okay?"

Her question was the same one sitting at the forefront of my mind right now. I wasn't feeling so great myself. My knees still wobbled, and I was beginning to wonder if my pulse would settle down. But taking care of Harp came first. She'd been through a terrifying experience and needed love and reassurance.

"He's at the hospital where the doctors and nurses will take care of him. He might come home later or have to stay overnight, but as soon as Mom knows something, she or Lex will call us."

The back door in the kitchen opened and closed, and my eyes widened. Gid coming home from work. I imagined the terror I'd feel if I walked into our kitchen right now without knowing what happened. I think I'd even left the water running in the sink.

"Mom! Dad!" Fear laced Gid's voice, and his heavy footsteps trailed through the hallway as he searched for our parents. For anyone.

I carried Harper to our parents' bed and sat her down. "Can you stay here for a minute, Harp? I need to talk to Gid."

She nodded and curled up against one of the pillows.

"Gid!" I hurried through the doorway.

He stopped at the foot of the stairs, and his head whipped in my direction. He had a harried, wild appearance, and his nostrils flared. "What happened? Who's hurt? Are they..." He wouldn't allow himself to say the words. Dead was final. Saying it made it real.

"It's Dad."

Gid sank into himself and grasped the newel post for support as he closed his eyes tightly.

I could have handled that better. "No! He's all right. I think. I don't know all the details yet, but he had a big gash on his arm and lost a lot of blood." Seemed like gallons of it if you looked at all the blood-soaked towels. "Mom and Lex took him to the emergency room. Harp's here with me. She's really scared after seeing Dad like that."

"Remind me to punch you in the face later for the way you scared me just now. Where is she?"

"In Mom and Dad's bedroom. I took her in their bathroom to clean her up. We should check on her." As I suspected, when we looked in on Harp, she was sound asleep on our parents' bed. After everything that happened, she was probably exhausted. I picked up a throw from one of the chairs and covered her with it. Gid ran upstairs and brought back Rex, Loki, and Percy to tuck under the blanket with her.

"We should clean up the kitchen," I said.

Gid nodded, and we headed there.

Even though I'd already seen it, my knees nearly buckled when I walked into the kitchen again. Knowing this was Dad's blood unnerved me. There was so much of it, and it was everywhere. While I tossed the bloody dishtowels into a trash bag and sanitized the counters and sink, Gid mopped the floor. It might not be up to Mom's standards, but at least it didn't look like a crime scene anymore. I texted Lex to see if there was any news. He said Mom was in with Dad and the doctor.

When Harp woke up, we made her macaroni and cheese and let her watch one of her favorite movies, her stuffed animals lined up on the sofa beside her. Gid and I stayed close in case she needed us. We might have used Harp as an excuse, but we all needed to be close right now. Dad suffered an injury, a serious one from my perspective, but we still didn't know what happened. Was it really an accident? Was Cora the cause of it?

I heard a car door slam outside. Only one. Gid and I dashed into the kitchen as Lex came in through the back door. He looked like a victim in a horror movie. Blood streaked his arms and part of one side of his face, and more than half of his shirt was stiff with dried blood.

"How is he?" Gid asked.

"There was muscle and tendon damage, and he had surgery to repair it. He's in a big cast and has a lot of physical therapy in his future. They're keeping him for at least a couple days. Mom wants to stay with him, so I'm taking some things back to the hospital for her."

"What happened?" I asked.

Lex sighed and pressed his palms against his eyes. Harp wasn't the only one who was exhausted. "We were using the circular saw in the garage cutting the boards to replace the damaged ones on the porch. Dad finished cutting the last one and turned off the saw. I'd stacked the wood and started to carry it out the door. When Dad went back to the saw table to grab his phone, it started up and put that gash in his arm."

"It turned back on?" Gid asked. "Maybe a malfunction?"

Lex's face paled. "That's the thing. It didn't turn on by itself, and there was no malfunction. I unplugged the saw myself before I picked up the wood. You know how strict Dad is about safety when using the power tools." Dad's rules were iron clad. Safety glasses, no headphones, no music, no goofing off. And make sure Harper wasn't around.

Fury clawed its way up my throat. "You think it was Cora?"

"Absolutely," Lex replied. "I think it was punishment for the spirits that crossed the veil. And a warning. She can get to us, any of us, at any time."

Gid clenched his jaw, his mouth a tight line. "She could have killed him. It's a miracle she didn't."

Time was running out. Cora gave us two weeks to find the daggers, and the clock was ticking. I swore it was ticking even faster now. "How's Mom?"

"Scared, but calm. You know how she is. I'm going to grab her things and get back to the hospital. Can you two take care of the mess in the garage?"

"No, I'll go," I said. "You take a shower and get some rest. Go hang out with Harp or something. But clean up first. Don't let her see you like this. She's scared enough." Lex nodded.

Gid nodded in agreement. "I'll take care of the garage."

"I don't think anyone should go out there alone. Maybe we should wait until tomorrow when all three of us can clean up," I suggested.

"I'll second that," Lex said. "But I'm tossing that circular saw into the yard. I'd hate to see either of you cut in half." Gid and I stared at him disapprovingly. "What? Too soon?"

"Way too soon," I said.

The mood shifted as we stood there and stared at each other in silence. For weeks we'd known about the Teller curse and killings courtesy of Cora, but this hadn't happened to distant relatives. We could have lost Dad today. It was too close and too real. And it wasn't nearly over.

Without a word being said, Gid pulled Lex and me in for a hug. We wouldn't mention it tomorrow or even next year because it wasn't our usual way. But it's what we needed right now.

CHAPTER SIXTEEN

I walked into Dad's hospital room and dropped the bag we'd packed for our parents onto a small table. Mom sat in a chair in the corner, the only light in the room coming from the cracked door leading into the bathroom. Her complexion was ashen, and dark crescents hung below her eyes. She stood, drew me in for a hug, and kissed my forehead. Dad was sleeping. A large white cast wrapped around his forearm. Harper would have a great time decorating it, but doing everyday activities would be awkward for him as long as he wore it. No piano lessons for Harper in the immediate future. His color was better. At least now he had more blood in his body than out. I hoped this picture would replace the last image I had of him covered in blood, passed out, and slung over Lex's shoulder as he carried Dad out the door. But I had a feeling that memory would stick with me for quite a while. Probably star in some nightmares. I walked over to the bed and held his hand for a moment before I left.

More medical bills, I thought as I walked back to the car. Knowing the mountain wasn't quite so massive anymore made me feel better. He was alive, and that's all that mattered. We all were. For how long, I didn't know.

When I got home and pulled the car around back, I noticed someone sitting on the patio. After locking the car, I found Gid and Aiden stretched out on the lounge chair. Gid's head rested on Aiden's shoulder, Aiden's arms wrapped around him, and their legs entangled. I took a seat on the chair across from them.

"He's asleep?" I whispered.

Aiden nodded. "Finally. It took a while. He told me what happened." He probably knew how the accident happened, but I doubted Gid had mentioned Cora in the conversation. "How's your dad?"

"Much better. He should be released tomorrow. Mom's spending the night at the hospital." I looked at Gid, his face free of worry lines, brows relaxed instead of scrunched into a scowl, and chuckled.

"What?" Aiden asked.

"It's nice to see Gid this way for a change instead of charging through life growling at people. Good idea about the tea. I doubt meditation is in his future, but he's been less like an angry wasp and more like—"

Aiden interrupted me. "You'd better not say butterfly. I might feel compelled to report that to him. Then the angry wasp would reemerge."

Thinking of Gid as a butterfly nearly made me snort.

"You're good for him, Aiden. He cares about you."

He turned his head toward Gid, who was still sleeping quietly. "Yeah, well, that goes both ways." By the soft expression on his face, I knew his feelings for my brother were genuine. I really hoped Gid didn't start his geese honk snoring. Aiden's feelings might take a turn in the other direction if he had to listen to that noise. He raised his head and looked at me. "I heard you've been spending time with that brunette from the beach."

I couldn't help the smile that slid across my face. Last night, Willow and I ran on the beach together again. We'd already run a couple miles when we stopped for a water break. The sky was streaked with shades of burnt orange and pink as we sat on the sand and sipped our water while watching the sunset.

"Quiz time. What does offsides mean?" Willow had started teaching me about soccer so I wouldn't be completely lost at her games after school started. It was going... not very well. My ability to understand sports was equal to my ability to play. As in none.

Sports had never interested me, so maybe my mind erected a barrier designed to ban that knowledge and focus my brainpower elsewhere. Like on useless bits of trivia. I knew Marie Curie's hundred-year-old belongings were still radioactive. *Mulan* had the highest kill-count of any Disney character. Apparently, my mind had a talent for remembering weird things I came across while reading. One of these days, I might be a valuable commodity in a trivia game. But recalling the names of soccer positions? My mind went blank.

"Isn't that when you break a rule and the ref makes you go stand off the side of the field?"

Willow rolled her eyes and smacked me on the shoulder. "Seriously?"

"I told you, Gid and Lex got all the sports genes. But ask them to name one book written by Jane Austen and all you'll get are deer-in-headlights expressions. Lex might ask if she was the woman who hung out with gorillas."

Willow giggle-snorted at my reply. Right then I decided her laugh rivaled Harp's. I loved hearing it.

"Why do I need to know the rules if all I'm doing is watching you?"

She turned toward me. Strands of hair that had escaped her ponytail blew across her face.

This time, my hand didn't ache to tuck them behind her ear. I actually did it. "Can I kiss you?"

Her lips curved with the smallest smirk. "Took you long enough to ask."

I gently touched my lips to hers, and the kiss was everything I'd hoped. When I pulled back, the promise I'd made to Everline replayed itself in my head. Willow and I could be more than friends, but I'd never bring her to the house until things were settled with Cora.

Gid hadn't made that promise. Aiden was here. He wasn't in the house, but I guess the patio counted. "Yeah. We've been seeing each other. Her name's Willow."

"Nice, Beck. Hope things work out. At least this one's real," he teased, referring to the conversation about Sophie being my fake girlfriend.

"Thanks." I stood and stretched. "Mom's going to be mad she missed you. She's been hounding Gid about inviting you to dinner for weeks."

Aiden tightened his arms around my brother. "That would be great. Hey, do you mind getting us a blanket? I don't want to wake him."

"Sure. Be right back." I was glad Aiden was there for Gid. He needed the support. But somehow, I felt like a mistake had been made.

•　•　•

"Beck, wake up!" Something poked me in the arm. It was a tiny, persistent something that continued to poke me without stopping. "Open your eyes!"

I cracked one eyelid open. A blurry Harper stood at the side of my bed, holding my glasses. She wore a baseball hat that was too large for her, which meant Lex had dressed her this morning. The art of styling a six-year-old girl's hair wasn't in his skill set, so he always plopped a hat on her head. He said it served the same purpose of keeping Harp's hair out of her face. The position of the sun on my wall told me it was later than when I normally got up. "What time is it?"

Harp shrugged. "I already had lunch, so it's after that." Between my late run to the hospital and everything that happened with Dad yesterday, I'd been too wired to sleep. The last thing I remembered was my phone saying 4:13 am. "There's a girl downstairs who wants to see you. She's pretty," Harp said, dragging out the last word in a sing-song voice.

I bolted upright in bed. "Downstairs?" She nodded, holding out my glasses. I took them from her and slid them on, then grabbed a t-shirt from the foot of my bed and pulled it over my head. It had to be Willow. She's the only girl I knew here, other than her friends, and there was no reason for them to come to my house. I'd texted Everline last night about Dad's accident, and she'd said to take the morning off.

Harp followed me out of my bedroom door and down the hallway. Halfway down the stairs, I remembered I was still wearing pajama pants. They'd have to do.

Willow stood in the foyer talking to Lex. And that made me nervous on so many levels. Her smile brightened as I came down the last few stairs. Then her gaze drifted to my hair. She covered her mouth and tried to hide her laughter. I knew what my hair looked like when I rolled out of bed. Her amusement was totally justified. Too late to do anything with it now. I had to own it.

"Love the hair, dude," Lex said. "Your girlfriend brought over flowers for Dad." He nodded toward a vase full of colorful carnations sitting on a table. "She also brought stuff from a bakery I already called dibs on. You snooze, you lose." He pulled a croissant from the bag labeled The Bun Also Rises. After taking way too big a bite, he walked toward the kitchen. Mouth still full, he called over his shoulder, "Nice to meet you, Willow. Glad you're not fake."

She looked at him questioningly, but then shrugged it off.

"Hey," I said, now conscious of my unbrushed teeth.

"I'm sorry about your dad's accident. Grandma told me about it when I brought her croissants to the bookstore this morning. I hope that's alright?"

"Yeah, of course."

Willow glanced over at Harp, who stood on the bottom stair watching us closely.

"Are you Beck's girlfriend?" she asked.

Between the pajama pants, the wild hair, morning breath, and now two comments about Willow being my girlfriend, I thought about going back upstairs, diving into bed, and covering my head. "I'm sorry, Willow. My sister's—"

"Yes, I am," Willow interrupted me. "If that's okay with him."

Warmth flooded my body. I loved her directness. "It's absolutely okay with me."

"Good." Harp began skipping through the hallway singing, "Beck's got a girlfriend."

I rubbed the back of my neck. "Um, that was Harper. Sorry about that."

"I'm not. I'm glad she brought it up. And I'm glad we agree." She stepped forward and kissed my cheek, then grabbed my hand and led me toward the parlor to sit down.

Macie sat at a table playing backgammon with the ghost of a woman. It was the same woman Lex had first seen in his bedroom the night he'd thought she was Mom picking up his clothes and putting a coaster underneath his soda can. Over the past weeks, we'd learned she did that a lot. We didn't know where they'd come from, but coasters were now plentiful around the house. If one wasn't used, you might see the glass lift on its own to be set back down on a coaster that magically appeared. Macie said her name was Elizabeth. She didn't care to talk to us much, but I knew she enjoyed puttering around the house. I'd come home many days after work to find the clean clothes I'd left in my laundry basket because I hadn't had time to deal with them had been folded neatly and put away in my chest or hung in the closet. Laundry and coasters were her thing. Elizabeth was pretty nice to have around, and Mom agreed. She liked seeing our clothes put away instead of us pulling clean clothes from the basket until they were all dirty again.

When Macie saw me with Willow, she raised her eyebrows, then gave a knowing smile. Elizabeth glanced over briefly, then turned back to the game. Willow gave no sign she saw them. Not that I expected her to. We took a seat on the same sofa where Macie had first appeared.

"Lex said your dad's going to be okay?"

"Yeah, I think he's being released today. It was scary for a while there. All that blood. And poor Harp. You wouldn't know by looking at her today, but she was terrified."

"I'm sure she was." Willow nodded sympathetically. "That's a lot for a little kid."

Macie and Elizabeth had continued their game, but I knew they were listening to us. Now that I'd gotten over the shock of Willow being here, my stomach plummeted when I remembered what I'd promised her grandmother. "Does Everline know you're here?"

"I don't think so. She told me about your dad when I dropped off her bakery bag at the bookstore this morning. I wanted to do something nice for you and your family. I knew where the Teller house was, so I just dropped by. Was that all right?" she asked, worry tingeing her voice.

"Definitely," I reassured her. "And thank you. Baked goods and flowers are always welcome. The croissants also kept Lex from sitting here and watching us every minute."

She laughed. But without the cute snort this time. "He's... entertaining. And also a flirt."

It wasn't my fault Willow came here on her own, but for Everline, at least I could stop Willow from staying here long. I really needed to grab some food and get down to the bookstore. "Thanks again for coming by. Harp's going to grill me about you the second you leave. She's probably hiding around the corner listening," I chuckled.

"I am not!" a voice from the hall said, and then I heard little feet running away.

We both laughed, then Willow stood. "I should let you get ready. Grandma said you were working this afternoon. Let me know if you need anything. Text me later?"

"I will." She tiptoed up, hugged me, then kissed me quickly.
I wanted it to be longer, but... morning breath.

"See you later, boyfriend."

I grinned so widely I was afraid my lip would split.

CHAPTER SEVENTEEN

I was still sleeping in the guest room down the hall from my bedroom. Sleeping was a stretch. It was the wee hours of the morning, but I lay in bed staring at the ceiling, arms behind my head. I'd been awake for hours tossing and turning. Gotta love insomnia.

Dad was home and recovering, but the thought of what could have happened to him was never far away. We'd come so close to burying another Teller in the cemetery. He'd paid the price for Harper helping the spirits to cross over. Who would Cora target the next time we did something wrong? What if she discovered Harper was responsible? When I thought of something happening to my sister, my mind hit a brick wall. Like I'd never see beyond that wall if she was gone.

Then there were the daggers. We desperately needed them. Their possible hiding places entered and exited my mind like a revolving door. I considered and discarded locations we'd already searched or were illogical. If we stood any chance of getting rid of Cora, finding them was a priority. They were the only barrier between us and death. Rows of graves in the family cemetery confirmed it.

Even if we found them, we didn't know the proper way to use them. How were we supposed to pull Iona's fragmented soul from them? If we figured that out, what did we do with them then? Would she be a spirit again? Could we kill Cora if we sank the blades into her? Was death immediate? Her first death hadn't taken, so if the opportunity to stab her presented itself, how could we be certain this one would finally send her to the next plane?

One step at a time, Beck.

Maybe tomorrow I could put Lex on researching the books for how the daggers work while Gid and I continued our search. I wasn't sure how thorough of a researcher Lex was, but he'd coasted his way through school with near perfect grades so far so he must possess some skills.

I rolled to my side and closed my eyes again. Didn't they say resting your body was almost as good as sleep? Not sure if I believed that. I tried breathing exercises and forced my body to relax. Just as I was beginning to drift off, the room seemed to brighten. I'm not ashamed to admit to sleeping with the bedside lamp on after some of the more disturbing things that happened in this house. It made me feel better if I woke from a nightmare. I'd probably left it on. And then I was fully awake. I was certain I hadn't left it on because just an hour ago I'd been staring outside at the scattered clouds that trailed across the full moon.

I opened my eyes. My bedroom door was open about a foot or so, and a soft light streamed in. Something creaked in the hallway. I bolted upright and watched as the bedroom door slowly creeped open inch by inch. I groped for my glasses on the nightstand beside me and put them on. My breath stopped, but my heart thumped wildly in my chest. Maybe one of my brothers figured out a location for the daggers. Or maybe it was Harper. Wouldn't be the first time she'd crawled into my bed after a nightmare.

"Gid? Lex?" Although I spoke barely above a whisper, my voice sounded unnaturally loud in the quiet night. But there was no response.

The door continued to open until it softly thumped against the stop. I peered into the darkness beyond in the hallway. Nothing was there. In houses this old, it wasn't unheard of for doors to open on their own, right? Houses settled like aged bones. Things shifted.

Just when my heart rate started to return to normal range, the hallway grew brighter. I blinked a few times. Maybe it was my imagination. But the light continued to intensify. I pushed the covers aside and swung my legs around to the side of the bed. I'd rather greet whatever was coming on my feet. It was easier to run if escape was required.

My fight or flight instinct activated, and I internally warred with myself over which to choose. Even if I chose to run, whatever created the light waited in the hallway. Jumping out my second-floor window wasn't an option. The decision was made for me. I inhaled deeply to steel my nerves and braced myself for battle.

A glowing white orb floating about four feet off the floor bobbed through the doorway of my room. It was smaller than a soccer ball but bigger than a baseball. It moved gently toward me then stopped a couple of feet away.

I stared in awe, unsure of what the orb was or what it wanted. When I slowly raised my hand toward it, the orb glided backward, just out of my reach. It didn't move aggressively, and I wasn't getting any threatening vibes from it. If anything, the light seemed gentle. Calming. It floated toward the door, then stopped, almost as if it was waiting for me. Maybe it was here to help. Should I follow it? I knew I'd never forgive myself if I didn't. It struck me that this could be related to Cora somehow. She'd crafted a trick that could hurt me or result in my death. But my gut told me she had no part in this, and I had to trust that instinct.

I picked up a t-shirt from the floor and quickly pulled it over my head, shoved my feet into shoes, then grabbed my phone from the nightstand. I stepped into the dark hallway. As I passed Gid and Lex's rooms, I thought about waking them, but shut that down. What if the orb didn't wait for me? What if it got spooked? That idea almost made me laugh. Do otherworldly balls of light get spooked?

Whatever this was, I didn't want to do anything to break the spell. Good or bad, I'd tag along wherever it led me.

I trailed it down the stairs, stepping around the creaky spots so I didn't wake anyone. Even though we'd only been here a short time, I'd memorized the noisy steps. That knowledge always came in handy when I needed to sneak out or back in after curfew. Not that those opportunities had arisen since we'd moved in.

We continued through the foyer then down the hallway leading toward the back of the house, passing the library to my right. The furniture cast eerie shadows against the wall as we passed. My neck hair prickled, and it felt like I was being watched. Considering other ghosts shared this home with us, it was entirely possible.

We entered the kitchen. Mom always kept the overhead stove light on at night. It did nothing to dampen the brightness of the orb. The ball floated through the room in the direction of the back door, which made me glad I'd worn shoes.

But we didn't go outside. Right before it reached the back door, the ball stopped at the entrance to the basement and hovered as it waited for me to catch up.

"Are we going to the basement?" I whispered. Not that I expected a verbal answer, but maybe some kind of sign of agreement. When the orb flashed once, I assumed that was my response.

I turned the knob and eased open the door leading to the creaky wooden stairs. Briefly I thought about opening the flashlight app on my phone, but the ball provided enough light that falling down the stairs and breaking my neck wasn't really a concern. The trail to wherever it was leading me was about to end. Unless there were hidden tunnels. Which is something I couldn't entirely rule out, considering all the secrets this house held.

I crept down the stairs behind the orb until we reached the packed dirt floor of the unfinished basement. Again, I was grateful I'd put on shoes. Who knew what was hidden in the bowels of our home? The rusty old freezer and ancient refrigerator shoved against the stone wall were perfect places to store dead bodies, and that didn't take the dark corners into consideration.

The orb took a sharp right turn at the bottom of the steps then stopped, though it continued bobbing in the air. I sensed movement under the staircase and spun in that direction.

A young girl crouched beneath them. She wore a white dress that looked decades old, her light hair trailing a few inches over her shoulders. Her eyes resembled dark, bottomless pits, and she clutched the same doll in her arms. I knew she wasn't alive and recognized her as the same girl from the other plane who warned me Cora was coming. My breath hitched, and I fought the instinct to run. She'd helped me before, and I assumed the orb led me to her for a reason.

She rose from her crouched position and glided slowly toward me.

A month ago, I'd have scrambled upstairs by now, roused my family, and herded everyone to the car to get the hell out of there. But now? This girl was far less threatening than other things I'd seen and experienced in this house.

Cold enveloped me as she drew closer, and my exhalations released puffs into the air. She tilted her head up, her black eyes focused on my face, and offered her hand as if she wanted me to take it. Shivering from the frigid air, I placed my warm hand into her icy one.

The orb followed us as we wound our way through a maze of storage boxes and old furniture. Who was this girl? With all the children's graves in the cemetery, I was certain her name was etched into one of them. Cora deserved to burn in hell for killing this kid and condemning her to this existence. It was tragic that her life had ended at such a young age, and she deserved to be at peace. Maybe Harper could help her find it.

When we reached the far back corner of the basement, she stopped. Stacks of cardboard boxes, some of them partially collapsed after so many years, lined the wall. The girl turned and pointed toward two side-by-side stacks that sat apart from the others. Her face tilted up to mine.

"Is there something in the boxes?" I asked in a low voice. She shook her head vigorously and gestured again. Not a lot of options here. "Is something behind the boxes?" The girl nodded, and the orb flashed brighter, seeming to agree with her.

My fingers were nearly numb from the cold when I pulled my hand from hers. I rubbed my hands together to get the blood flowing again, otherwise my numb digits would be useless. These boxes weren't piled as high as some others, and I could easily reach the top of the two stacks. None were very heavy, and I had no trouble moving them to the floor.

Once I'd cleared the space, I stood in front of a brick wall. No secret doorways or hidden crevices like I'd expected to find. No signs reading "Hidden Daggers Here" with a flashing arrow pointing to the exact location. It was just a wall.

I looked at the girl. "Is this what you wanted me to find?"

She nodded.

I inspected the wall closer. This is what the girl wanted me to find, so I must be missing something. Running my hands over the bricks, I felt for indentations or levers. Anything that could help with my search.

The girl placed her icy hand on my forearm and shook her head. She pointed to a specific spot on the wall about five feet high. I shone my cellphone's flashlight where she directed and took a few steps back to get a better view.

Then I saw it.

If the girl hadn't shown me this specific spot, it would have gone unnoticed. The bricks were a lighter shade than the others. Now I wondered how I'd missed it. With symmetrical rows and evenly spaced bricks surrounding that area, the craftmanship of the original bricklayer was evident. But one section was different. Those bricks were slightly crooked with splattered mortar freckled across them, almost as if the person who'd laid them had little time for accuracy.

I grinned. Something must be hidden behind the bricks, and I really hoped it was the daggers. I just needed a tool to break through the wall.

With my phone flashlight app and the orb lighting the way, I searched the basement. We'd established my relatives rarely tossed out anything. Surely there were tools among all the storage boxes and antique furniture. I searched high and low, lifted sheets covering furniture and opened chests containing old clothing, not really expecting to find the tools there, but I didn't want to leave any stone unturned. This was too important. Just feet away from the stairs I'd descended earlier, I found a pickaxe standing in a corner, along with rakes and brooms. Perfect. I hurried back over to the wall where the young girl still waited, the orb trailing behind me.

Lifting the pickaxe over my shoulder, I drove it into the brick wall over and over. It would be a miracle if I didn't wake anyone, but two floors separated me and my family, and I hoped that was enough insulation. Sweat covered my brow and the back of my neck from physical exertion, but I didn't have to work long before the bricks fell away to reveal a small door.

It measured about two square feet, and I noted it seemed to be made of iron. From my research, I knew iron was an element that weakened spirits and sometimes drove them away. Even the young ghost girl kept her distance, and we weren't a threat to each other. But with other not-so-friendly spirits, iron offered a person protection, at least in certain situations. I assumed it also protected whatever was behind this door and was added as an extra precaution.

Correction. Behind this *locked* door, which I discovered when my efforts to pull it open didn't budge it an inch. I turned back to the girl. "How do I open it? Can you help me?"

She lifted a chain hidden beneath the neck of her white gown over her head. Her small hands dropped it into mine. At the end of the chain was a tarnished brass key that looked as if it had been around for years. It was heavier than a normal key and had elaborate, interlocking designs along its stem.

"Thank you." I turned back toward the iron door, inserted the heavy key into the lock, then turned it. A groan pierced the silence, sounding almost like I'd awakened a metal monster from a decades-long slumber.

The door creaked open, but darkness cloaked whatever lay inside, and I was more than a little nervous about putting my hand in there when I didn't know what waited in the abyss.

The flashlight app had drained my phone's power. The battery icon had turned red, then my screen went dark. I looked at the glowing orb and cocked an eyebrow.

It seemed to understand exactly what I needed and floated closer to the opening, casting light into the iron encasement. A black, dust-covered square case lay inside.

I lifted it out. It was heavier than I'd expected. Layers upon layers of dust coated the lid. Trying to blow it clean only resulted in me sneezing. I set the black case on top of one of the storage boxes and used my sleeve to wipe it off. Gold lettering decorated the lid.

Teller Family.

Whatever was inside this box, and I assumed it must be the daggers, had been in my family for generations. I turned my gaze to the ghost girl and the orb of light. They still didn't speak, and maybe they couldn't, but both seemed quietly supportive. Placing my quivering hands on either side of the lid, I slowly lifted it.

I gasped, filled with a mixture of shock and awe.

Our search had come to an end.

Nestled inside a black velvet lining were three daggers. The holy grail we'd been searching for over the past several weeks. Weapons hidden in a place that had eluded our relatives for decades. Our key to defeating Cora.

A silver-tipped black sheath encased each blade. Intricately woven, Celtic knots formed the hilts, and the top of each hilt held a different gemstone—amethyst, ruby, and sapphire. They sparkled beneath the orb's light, and I wondered if the colors signified anything. My hand trembled slightly as I gently ran my fingers over the weapons. After being locked behind a brick wall in the basement for over a century, they were frigid to the touch.

I picked up the ruby dagger and unsheathed it, turning it side to side. The silver blade glinted in the light. Its weight felt steady in my hand. I resheathed it then returned it to the case. The sapphire dagger felt similar in my hands, and I marveled at the craftmanship.

My reaction to the amethyst dagger was entirely different. The second I wrapped my fingers around the hilt, a surge of power shot up my arm. I dropped the dagger and staggered back in shock, nearly toppling over a tower of storage boxes behind me. My heart galloped as I gulped in a breath and regained my balance. I guess that reaction answered my question. Clearly, the different colored stones were significant, and the amethyst one was meant for me. Would Gid and Lex have the same reactions with their daggers? I had to believe they would and should probably warn my brothers about the power surge before they started fighting over them. They may not be wands, but in this case, the blade chose the wielder.

This time I was prepared as I reached for the dagger again. Power flowed up my arm, but I gripped the hilt tightly. Clutching the sheath with my left hand, I pulled the blade free. According to the book I'd found, the blades were made of iron. Dagger knowledge wasn't stored in my wheelhouse, but there was no doubt in my mind these were valuable and powerful.

The ghost girl and ball of light were still with me, and I turned in their direction. "Thank you. These give us a chance to save our family and help you cross over. But then you must have known that, or you wouldn't have led me here."

The orb flashed brighter.

"I promise we'll do everything we can to help all of you. You have my word."

I sheathed the weapon once more and placed it back on the bed of velvet. After closing the dusty box, I tucked it under my arm. The young girl and the orb came closer and blocked my path back to the stairs. I stepped to the right to go around them, and they moved to block me again. I got the message. They didn't want me to leave the basement with the daggers.

A light bulb went off in my head. Duh. Of course. The case was hidden behind this wall years ago for a still unknown reason I hoped came to light soon. For now, it should remain here until we knew more. At least we finally had the daggers.

I returned the box to where I'd found it, then closed the door and locked it. I slipped the chain holding the key over my head and tucked it inside my t-shirt. I'd bring Gid and Lex down here tomorrow morning. The daggers would choose them, and then we'd learn how to use them. I hoped somehow the skills our family possessed over so many generations were passed down genetically or their spirits could assist us in some way.

Now that we had them, Cora would show herself soon.

Time was running out.

CHAPTER EIGHTEEN

"A ball of light led you down here." Gid folded his arms as he leaned against the basement wall, ankles crossed. I'd woken him and Lex early this morning, anxious to show them the daggers and to get started on learning how to use them. In return, I'd received a pillow to the head from Lex and a long stream of mumbled swear words from Gid. If Harp hadn't still been asleep, he absolutely wouldn't have mumbled them.

Lex looked at me doubtfully. "And a ghost girl waited under the basement stairs." His eyes tracked a male spirit who'd emerged from the wall beside where Gid leaned. The man paid us no attention as he passed by and continued up the basement steps toward the kitchen. It had gotten to the point where we no longer gawked when we encountered the ghosts because it had become the norm. Our abilities seemed to have grown. Seeing and communicating with the spirits no longer required us to be together.

"Come on, you guys can't be surprised by any of this." I gestured to the direction the ghost guy had taken. "The spirits in this house far outnumber us living humans, in case you haven't noticed. And we finally have the daggers. That's the important thing."

"What did the girl look like? Did she creep you out? Give you nightmares for the rest of the night? I bet you screamed, right? You totally screamed," Lex said.

"I didn't scream, okay?" I pushed up my glasses. "It was the same young girl who warned me Cora was coming when I was in the other plane."

"And she brought you the key?" Gid asked.

I nodded. "She must have heard me asking for William, Mary, or Joseph Teller and then looked for them. Or maybe she already knew where they were. However it went down, she's given us the chance to protect ourselves."

Gid wiped his face then pushed his hands up through his hair. His didn't look much better than Lex's. "Well, let's see them."

I pulled the key from beneath my shirt, opened the iron door, then withdrew the black box holding the daggers. After setting it on a storage box, I lifted the lid to reveal the jeweled weapons nestled in the black velvet lining. A ray of sunlight through a narrow basement window chose that moment to fall across them. The amethyst, ruby, and sapphire glowed brightly.

Lex gasped in awe. "You weren't kidding, Beck. They look... otherworldly."

Gid pushed off the wall and moved closer. "And one of those daggers chooses us?"

I nodded. "The ruby and sapphire ones had no effect on me. I might as well have picked up a butter knife in the kitchen. But the second I touched the amethyst blade, it was like being electrocuted."

Lex slowly reached his hand toward the ruby dagger, the one closest to him, and touched the Celtic knotted hilt. He raised his head and looked at Gid and me. "Nothing. I don't feel anything."

"Try the sapphire one," I said. If it had no effect on him, maybe Macie had been wrong about the three siblings. Or maybe *we* were the wrong siblings since we'd descended from a different branch of the family. If that was the case, I didn't know where we'd go from here.

Lex lifted the sapphire dagger from the case, and his reaction was immediate. Tremors shot up his arm. His bedhead hair rose into the air as if he'd touched a Van de Graaff generator. Everything returned to normal—in this case, his regular bedhead—when he released his grip and gently placed the dagger back into the case.

Lex's eyes were wide. "If I wasn't awake before, I am now. Yeah, so I'll be claiming the blue one." He blinked hard. "Figures the ruby one would be yours, Gid. Matches your fiery temper."

Gid snarled at Lex before lifting the ruby dagger from the case. His grip tightened around the hilt. Nothing happened. His gaze shot to mine in question. Then his head fell back, and his eyes rolled until the whites showed. Similar to the reactions Lex and I had, Gid's arm vibrated from the power of the dagger. Slowly his head lifted, his eyes returned to normal, and he hurriedly placed the weapon back into its slot in the case.

Gid wiped his mouth with the back of his hand as he stared at the daggers that would hopefully be our salvation. He lifted his gaze first to Lex and then me. "So, what's next? I'm ready to get started."

"Beck, did you see this?" I turned in Lex's direction to see him pulling a thin, black leather book from the daggers' hiding place. It must have been lying beneath the case. He blew dust from its cover, causing me to sneeze, then set it on the boxes beside the daggers. Gid and I moved closer to get a better look.

"I was so excited about finding the daggers that I must have missed it last night." I sniffled then opened the book. Cursive handwriting filled the page, and the date at the top was September 8th, 1923. "It looks like a journal." I picked up the book and sat on a hideous lime green sofa in the corner to study it. Books were my thing, so Gid and Lex left me to it.

Scanning the first couple pages, I quickly understood why the daggers had been hidden and locked away. My stomach sank as I continued reading. The author had signed his name after the last paragraph: William Teller. I slumped back against the sofa. My body was limp, and I felt like throwing in the towel and calling it quits. I'd gone from the high of thinking we finally had the upper hand over Cora to reading William's journal and discovering the truth.

He'd done the right thing in hiding the daggers. There was no way we could use them.

"What is it, Beck?" Lex asked. "You look like you witnessed a book burning."

"It's bad, isn't it," Gid said.

"Worse than you could imagine. Sit down."

Gid and Lex pulled over two rickety dining room chairs that had seen better days.

"Doesn't it give instructions on how to bring Iona back? Is it a weird ritual where we have to dance naked around a fire while we wear animal skins?" Lex asked. "I want it on record that I'll only dance naked with you two if all other options are exhausted."

I lacked the energy to deal with Lex's attempts at humor at the moment and let it fall to the wayside. "The journal was written by William Teller. There's a way to reunite Cora with Iona, and he detailed every step."

Gid leaned forward, elbows on his knees. "But that's a good thing, right?"

I shook my head. "The pieces of her soul can be drawn from the daggers, but they have to be rejoined inside a living person." Gid and Lex looked at me in confusion. "That person would die, and Iona would take over their body. The same with Cora. Whoever she possesses would die." I swallowed hard. "That's why William and his siblings hid the daggers. They couldn't kill innocent people and didn't want any future Tellers to be tempted."

The two of them were quiet as the meaning of this discovery sank in. Cora had demanded we reunite her with Iona to end the curse. If we didn't succeed, our family died.

Gid broke the silence first. "I get it. It's the Teller family curse, and no one else needs to be dragged into it. It's our responsibility."

Lex looked thoughtful, then presented a truly demented idea. "Okay but consider this. What if we got someone who's really unlikable? Iona could take over her body. Don't look at me that way, Gid, hear me out. There's this girl who works at Joe's and she's rude to the customers, mean to the other servers, and yells at the kitchen staff when her order is delayed. No one likes her, and we'd all be happier without her. I'm just saying, we could make the world a better place."

I stared at him for a long moment. "Sacrificing your coworker's life to bring back a child who murders people wouldn't make the world a better place. Besides, do you actually think you could live with the guilt of killing her?"

Lex narrowed his eyes as if considering his answer before he replied. "I'm pretty sure I could bury the guilt down deep and survive just fine. Seriously, Gid, quit looking at me like that. Your eyebrows will grow together. Do you really want to go through life with a unibrow?"

Gid's jaw ticked.

Lex sighed heavily. "Fine. We'll put my idea on the backburner for now."

Defeat hung heavy in the air, and we sat together quietly as if already mourning our loss. I felt frustrated and helpless. We'd thought finding the daggers would solve our problems. End the curse that had decimated our family tree. Sacrificing innocent people to give Cora her daughter never crossed my mind. Breaking this curse was the most important thing in the world to me, but it was unconscionable to kill another family's loved one to save my own.

The thought of which one of us would be the first to die crossed my mind, and I immediately crushed it. It was a pain too great to bear. If the thought of losing my brothers hurt that much, I couldn't imagine the reality of it. Thinking about Harper taking one of our places was even worse. It stole the breath from my lungs and the strength from my limbs.

"So, we're back to square one," Lex said. "Back to waiting for Cora to kill us one by one."

Gid vaulted out of the rickety chair and kicked it against the basement wall where it shattered into pieces. Lex and I ducked and shielded our eyes. "No. I refuse to give up. None of us is dying, okay? There's got to be another way." His nostrils flared as he breathed heavily and started pacing. "We have the daggers now, so why do we think giving Cora her daughter is the only way to save us? Let's start talking about killing Cora."

"Other generations of Tellers tried for years, Gid. Now they're buried in the family cemetery, and she's still here," I said.

Gid stopped pacing and stared at me in disbelief. "So you're just going to roll over and give up? Wait to die? What about us? What about Harper?"

His words stabbed me like a knife in the heart. None of us asked for this curse. We'd inherited it because Klaus, Karl, and Hans Teller tried to do the right thing by ending Iona's killing spree. Maybe those before us armed with the daggers weren't strong enough to kill Cora. Most generations didn't possess the daggers to help them. The odds were never on their side.

But they weren't us. And they didn't have a fourth sibling to fight for. A little sister gifted with the ability to help the cursed Teller spirits still walking this earth to cross over and find peace. We had to fight.

"We do nothing, we die," Lex said. "If we try to kill her the outcome may be the same, but at least we tried. I'm not sitting around waiting for Cora to take a weed eater to my skull or rip out my internal organs and use my rib cage as a lobster trap."

I grimaced. "Those are oddly specific ways to die."

"Study those books again, Beck, and see if you can figure out where the other Tellers went wrong. We'll help you," Gid said. "We can't just give her what she wants. Not after everything she's done. Cora doesn't get a happily ever after."

CHAPTER NINETEEN

Macie still didn't know we'd found the daggers, and it was information she needed. After all, if it hadn't been for her, we'd probably have never known about them. Thanks to her, I'd found the family history books in the library that led us to discovering William was responsible for hiding the daggers. We were eager to tell Macie, it was just that none of us had come across her. We'd chalked it up to her traveling through different planes or times, as she'd mentioned the spirits did. Patience in locating her was required, and it wasn't something I had a lot of these days.

After breakfast one morning, I swung by the parlor where we'd first met Macie on the outside chance she might be there. Thanks to Harper, the spirit population had thinned, but I still passed more than a few in the hallway. None of them paid me any mind. Some muttered to themselves, a couple talked to people I couldn't see, and others carried out acts they would have performed while living in their time—mundane tasks like reading a newspaper, writing letters, or drinking tea from an elaborate service I'd seen on display a few times in the parlor. Outside we'd seen spirits visiting with each other on the porch, playing badminton or croquet in the yard, or strolling through the garden. Our parents still couldn't see them, but they'd become an everyday fixture to Gid, Lex, Harper, and me. Kind of like furniture around the house. I'd even dodged some in the kitchen while they prepared their meals. Not literally, of course. Harper added additional seats for her ghostly friends to the dining table regularly. Now we all understood they weren't imaginary friends.

I entered the doorway of the parlor to find Macie sitting at her usual table playing a game of backgammon with Elizabeth.

"Beck, how lovely to see you," Macie said.

Elizabeth looked at me, probably to see if I was carrying a drink, then stood and strolled out of the room. She brushed against me as she passed, and goosebumps rose on my arms from the chill.

"Thanks for folding my clothes yesterday, Elizabeth."

She stopped, glanced over her shoulder at me and nodded once, then continued toward the kitchen.

I took her abandoned chair across the table from Macie.

"What's put that big smile on your face this morning, Beck?"

"I have good news. We did it, Macie. We found the daggers."

She clutched at her pearls in excitement. "Oh, Beck! This is wonderful news! But how did you do it? Plenty have tried, but no one ever came close to locating them."

I recounted how I'd crossed to another plane and asked for help in locating William, Mary, or Joseph Teller. I told her about the little girl who'd warned me about Cora, and how Cora had nearly killed me before Gid found me. "The next night I followed a glowing white ball into the basement where the same young girl waited for me. She led me to the daggers and gave me a key to unlock the door where William hid them."

"A young girl?" Macie asked softly. Her expression seemed... hopeful. "Can you describe her?"

"She's older than Harper, around nine or ten years old, I think. Long white dress, blonde hair a little past her shoulders. She carried a doll with her."

Macie's eyes glistened as her hand flew to her mouth. If spirits could cry, she was on the verge of it.

Her reaction worried me. "Macie? Are you alright?"

Hand still covering her mouth, she nodded, but then dropped it to the table. "It's my Emily. My daughter. Our paths have never crossed, even though I've searched for her over the past year. I desperately miss all three of my children, but Emily was just a child when Cora took her. She never grew into a woman, or even a teenager. She was only ten when she died."

Macie was as solid as any of my family, and I reached across the table and took her frigid hand in mine. "I'm so sorry. It's unfair that I've encountered her twice now, and you haven't seen her at all. She's helped us so much. If she hadn't warned me about Cora when I went through the doorway, the outcome might have been completely different. Thanks to her, we have a chance against Cora. We're all grateful for her help."

Macie nodded, her face beaming with pride, but also sorrow.

"If I see Emily again, I'll tell her you've been looking for her."

"Please tell her I miss her and love her so much. I can only hope we'll be together soon."

Then I remembered something else Macie needed to know. "Maybe sooner than you think. We found out Harper has been helping spirits cross over. For years we thought she'd been making up imaginary friends, but it turns out she's helped spirits before we ever moved to this house. She could help you, Emily, and everyone left here when this is all over. Even before, if that's what you wanted."

Macie gaped at me in shock, her mouth hanging open. It was the most out of character expression I'd seen from her usual prim and proper demeanor. "Harper?" The hand I wasn't holding went back to the pearls. "I don't understand. She's just a child."

"It's a mystery to us, too. Lex noticed there'd been fewer spirits hanging around, and Harper overheard us. She explained the spirits had asked her for help, and she opened the door that took them to what she calls the good place. Like it was the simplest explanation in the world and something that happened every day."

Macie looked thoughtful. She pulled her hand away and clasped both of them together, the tips of her index fingers at her lips.

"From the investigator's reports, I remember Harper was born prematurely. Is that correct?"

"Yeah. I still remember how scary it was. We thought we'd lost her, and that's why Mom calls her our miracle baby."

"You thought you'd lost her? What do you mean by that?"

Harper was alive and well and healthy, but even talking or thinking about that time still hurt. I didn't want to exist in a world that didn't include her. "She was clinically dead for two minutes, but the medical staff revived her." My breath hitched even as I said it.

Macie smiled and nodded as if the pieces had fallen into place. "That explains it. Harper crossed over before as an infant. She's visited the other side, but probably has no memory of it. She's a kind of psychopomp."

I shook my head in confusion. This was an unfamiliar term to me. "A what?"

"Harper has the ability to open doors and escort spirits to the afterlife."

I slumped back against the chair. How she'd learned to "bring the light" as Harper said was a mystery to us. We'd accepted we would probably never find an answer. But here it was. Because she'd been dead herself for slightly less than two minutes, my sister possessed the ability to help spirits find peace. Whether the spirits remained here for unfinished business, attachment to a loved one, or a variety of other reasons—even if they were trapped here like our ancestors—she offered them the chance to move on. Harp was only six years old and probably didn't completely understand the immeasurable gift she gave them. She truly was a miraculous little girl.

Amazing as this discovery was, I had to relay the bad news to Macie. "There's a reason William Teller hid the daggers. The pieces of Iona's soul can be reunited, but not without a cost. Her spirit will permanently reside in another person's body. That person would die. William locked away the daggers so no one in the family would be tempted to bring innocent people into Cora's curse."

The hopeful expression on Macie's face slowly faded away with my words.

"Someone has to die to end this?"

I nodded.

"You're not considering—"

"Absolutely not."

Macie looked relieved.

"No one outside the family is getting dragged into this. We're working on another way. Cora can't win."

· · ·

"I've given you two weeks, and that's more than enough time."

It was late, after midnight, and Gid, Lex, and I were on the patio wondering how to reach Cora when she suddenly appeared in all her evil, decaying glory. Like she'd known we needed to speak to her. Right before she appeared, there was a disturbance in the air. It felt staticky and oppressive. As if an unseen force held us in place, and we couldn't move if we'd wanted.

That didn't stop me from swallowing a yelp of surprise when she materialized five feet away. Lex let out a weird sort of squeak snort and nearly fell out of his chair. But Gid stood tall and steady, arms crossed, glaring at her. He wouldn't give Cora the satisfaction of seeing his fear.

Cora fixed her gaze on me now, and I tried not to think about how quickly she could end my life. "You have news for me?"

"We found the daggers," I said, a slight tremor in my voice.

"I want to see them." Her murderous eyes gleamed with excitement.

"Not a chance," said Lex. "Even if we told you where they were, you couldn't get to them."

Cora lurched in Lex's direction, stopping only a foot away. He jerked backwards so quickly the front legs of his chair raised into the air before settling on the concrete patio again.

She cackled at his reaction.

"Would you bet your life on that?"

He shook his head quickly from side to side.

"I didn't think so." She turned back to me. "That's more than I expected from you. Do you know how to extract my daughter's soul from the blades?"

I tightened my grip on the arms of the chair to prevent my hands from shaking. "We need a vessel to reunite the pieces of Iona's soul." I swallowed hard. Surely everyone heard it. "A person. That person will die when Iona's soul merges, and she takes over their body."

"Are you volunteering?" Cora asked.

Gid stepped forward, arms still folded over his chest. "He's not. We're not. For this to work, you need all three of us. We're each connected to one dagger. If something happens to Lex, Beck, or me, your shot at getting Iona back is gone forever. The same goes for our parents and Harper. If you touch any of them again, the deal is off."

Cora seethed as she glared at Gid. She looked as if it took all her restraint not to cut Gid down where he stood. I doubt anyone had spoken to her like that since, well, since Klaus, Karl, and Hans. She didn't like playing by anyone else's rules, and it showed.

"Someone must die for Iona to live again. You're telling me you're fine with killing a person to end this curse?" Cora studied each of us, doubting our word.

We desperately needed to make her believe what we said.

"We'll do whatever's needed to protect our family," Gid replied, his expression stony. "That's all that matters." There was no hint of dishonesty on his face, no tell at all.

By all appearances, our plan was working. Gid didn't back down, and Cora seemed to believe him. Her all-consuming desire to see her daughter again could override any suspicion she felt. I hoped that was the case.

"I offered these same terms to William when he was alive. Bring Iona back and I'd end the curse. I suppose that explains why he hid the daggers so long ago. He and his siblings knew a sacrifice was required, and they didn't have the stomach for it. I suppose they weren't as heartless as you three."

A thought occurred to me, and I wondered why it had taken this long. "What if one of the Tellers had volunteered to allow Iona to take over their body? Someone that wasn't one of the siblings?"

"I would *never* allow my daughter to inhabit a descendent of the brothers responsible for her death," Cora said angrily. "I meant it as a threat when I asked you earlier. To even consider that option is an insult to Iona." Her vehement reaction made me think another Teller must have tried doing just that at some point. It was a viable idea and kept the curse within the family. But Cora wasn't having it. Also, it was one less person she had the pleasure of killing.

"No need to worry," Lex said. "Besides being heartless, we're also not that selfless. All we're concerned about is our family making it through this to the other side." Lex paused, then raised his hands in a surrendering motion. "Not the veil. I didn't mean the veil." He needed to shut up before Cora became suspicious. He was overselling it.

Cora stared hard at Lex, almost as if she was peering inside him, testing his honesty. He shifted in his seat uncomfortably. She looked at Gid. "I want it done tomorrow at midnight. If you don't show or if something goes wrong, one of you dies. Maybe all of you."

"You're not in control here. Remember what I said. If one of us dies, you'll never get Iona back. Only we can wield the daggers." Gid growled the words with a threatening smirk on his face. "Keep that in mind."

Cora glowered at him. Her hatred for us, for all the Tellers, was palpable. I felt it coming off her in waves. She terrified me. How had she fooled Harper into believing she was a loving, grieving mother who'd been separated from her daughter after they'd died? Just the thought of Cora being that close to Harp made me feel like someone scooped out all my internal organs.

No matter what, we couldn't fail tomorrow night. We had too much to fight for. Not just us, but all our own potential descendants. If any of us survived.

"Tomorrow at midnight here under the moon," Cora said, before disappearing.

The clock was ticking.

CHAPTER TWENTY

We had twenty-four hours. At this this time tomorrow night we could be dead or alive. Still pinned beneath the curse or free of it. Whatever the outcome, I knew we'd fight until our last breath.

Gid stared at the floor, deep in thought, as he leaned against the desk in the hidden room in the garage. I flipped through old paranormal case files. The Tellers had taken down so many spirits. There had to be something we could use, some technique we'd missed. The journals stated a spirit's strength directly correlated to their age and the number of deaths they'd caused. Knowing Cora posted off the chart numbers in both categories was disheartening and terrifying. Sure, we had the daggers, but we needed more. Cora believed we'd deliver a new "home" for Iona's spirit tomorrow night, someone whose body she could inhabit. When she learned we'd fooled her and had no intention of sacrificing anyone, we expected a full-on war.

"Anyone have a plan?" Lex asked. He'd turned the desk chair around backwards and straddled it. "Because I sure don't. Other than staying alive, anyway. I feel like we need a better plan than that."

Gid lifted his gaze from the floor and spoke with a confidence that almost set my mind at ease. "I may have one. When she realizes we don't have a body for Iona, we need to be prepared to fight immediately. That moment before she understands could give us a slight advantage. It may only be a split second, maybe two, but it's something." A couple months ago, Gid's response to this situation would have been to come out swinging, the quicker we responded the better. Now he'd stepped back, assessed the situation, and considered options. He'd taken on a leadership role, and I was more than happy to let him. My strengths leaned toward research and books. Gid's background in captaining his various varsity teams better equipped him to form a strategic plan to defeat Cora.

"To do what?" Lex asked. "Attack? Run? Pray? Curl up in the fetal position and hope for the best? I need direction, guys."

Gid swept his hand toward the shelves on either side of the room. "Look around us. We're surrounded by weapons used by the Tellers before us. The EMF meters are no help, but we've got holy water, blessed ropes, salt, and salt guns."

I looked up from the files I studied. "If she shows up and sees us with all this, she'll know right away we tricked her."

"I've thought of that," Gid said. "We tie the ropes around our waists and hide them under our shirts. We put salt in our pockets and in bags tied to our belt loops. Since we're meeting outside, we stash the salt guns in bushes. Pour holy water into spray bottles and set them around the patio. All these resources can be utilized to get Cora into a position for us to kill her with the daggers. From all the research and reading of the files, we know how other Tellers used them. Now we just need to plan and practice."

"When did you do all this thinking?" Lex asked, the corner of his mouth upturned in a smirk. "Just imagine what you could have done if you'd used your powers for good sooner."

Gid rolled his eyes and flipped off Lex. Some things never changed. "Grab some equipment and meet me outside. We've got a lot to do in the next twenty-four hours."

For the next several hours, we worked with the supplies from the hidden room and readied them for battle. My rope skills lacked finesse and would never garner me a future in cattle roping, but practice made me more confident. I tossed a loop around Lex a few times when he wasn't paying attention. He wasn't amused. Worse, I knew Cora wouldn't lose focus like that. Still, I was improving.

We'd retrieved the daggers from their iron enclosure in the basement and practiced wielding them until they felt comfortable. More like extensions of our hands. The spirits of other Tellers gathered around the yard and watched us. Some even offered pointers, which we gladly welcomed.

In the early morning hours, we woke our parents and told them about the deadline tonight. Mom sobbed uncontrollably. Dad cried quietly while he tried to comfort Mom and hug us at the same time. With Harper's bedroom upstairs, a floor separated us, and she hopefully wouldn't wake up. The thoughts of what faced us tonight paralyzed them with terror, but we all agreed they shouldn't be here. Cora could reach us anywhere, we knew that. Still, it eased our minds to know our parents and Harper wouldn't be close. They decided to take her to an amusement park, larger than the one on the pier, a couple hours from here. If Harper asked about going home, they'd use the distance as an excuse to spend the night. The plan was to tell her my brothers and I had to work, so we couldn't go. Anything to get her away from the house and out of immediate danger.

There was also that little detail Macie had mentioned. If one of us died, Harper took our place. Yeah. Not happening.

A few hours later, after the car was packed and they were ready to leave, the five of us tried to hold it together for Harper's sake as we stood in the driveway saying our goodbyes. To her, this was a day filled with rides, games, and maybe a new stuffed animal to add to her collection. For us, it was a day filled with uncertainty. Mom and Dad knew they could come home tomorrow to find their three sons dead. They may even face the same fate themselves. Gid, Lex, and I wondered if this was the last time we'd see our parents and sister. If Harp suspected anything was wrong, she might not want to leave us, so we all put on brave faces. Hugs were long and fierce, and promises and words of love were whispered between us and our parents. Mom's lips quivered nonstop, but she maintained control for the most part.

"I wish you could come," Harp said as I picked her up for a goodbye hug.

"Me too. You know how I love to race you on the carousel."

She giggled in my ear.

Lex pulled her from my arms. "My turn."

Harp rubbed her hands against the shaved sides of his head.

"Let's make your hair purple next time."

"You got it, girl." Lex looked over Harp's shoulder at me as he hugged her, his eyes glistening.

I knew exactly how he felt.

"Now me." Gid lifted Harper from Lex's arms. When her back was to Lex, he discreetly wiped his eyes with his shirt sleeve.

"Don't scratch me with your beard, Gid. Can I do your nails again when we get home?"

"Sure. Use as many colors as you want." He hugged her tightly, then buckled her in her booster seat in the car.

Harper had owned her brothers since the day she was born. Keeping her safe and ensuring Cora never touched her was a sacrifice we'd willingly make. No matter the consequences.

Dad and Mom took Gid, Lex, and me out of Harp's range of hearing. "This is wrong," Dad said, a pained shadow crossing his face. "A father shouldn't saddle his sons with this responsibility. It should be me battling Cora, not you three."

"None of us has a choice. This is the way it has to be," I said.

"And you still can't do anything with that right hand," Lex pointed out. Other than during his physical therapy appointments, Dad's arm and hand were immobilized for a while. It was awkward, but he'd had to use his left hand for most everyday tasks.

"We have a plan," Gid said. "Knowing the three of you are safe allows us to focus on it."

Dad nodded reluctantly, then hugged each of us and got in the car.

Mom had her turn with hugs next. "Promise you'll call."

We all nodded.

"If I don't hear from you, I'll know..." Her face grimaced in misery, and I could tell she was an inch away from losing it.

So were we. I swallowed a sob threatening to climb up my throat.

She wiped her eyes, then put on a smile, and headed toward the car. "Are you ready, Harp?" She slid in behind the wheel as Dad's restrictions also included driving. Mom was currently, and for weeks to come, his designated chauffeur.

Harp's stormy gray eyes met mine right before Mom closed the back door. Her face didn't shine with anticipation over carnival rides and sticky cotton candy. Instead, it was clouded over with suspicion and wariness.

CHAPTER TWENTY-ONE

Late that afternoon, we took a few hours to sleep. I'm not sure if any of us actually did, but our bodies needed rest. After all these years we finally had our own rooms, but by an unspoken decision we went to Gid's room. Gid and I took his bed, and Lex spread a blanket on the floor for himself. We faced an uncertain future, and I think the three of us felt the need to be together. No matter how much time we had left.

We ate a late dinner. A container of Mom's spaghetti sauce and meatballs was left over in the fridge. Lex boiled the pasta, I made a salad, and Gid baked garlic bread. If this was my last meal, I couldn't have asked for a better one. Our normally raging appetites were absent, but we needed fuel for what was coming. We forced down as much food as we could, and I savored every bite. Funny how food tastes so much better when you believe it might be the last time you'll eat it.

Other than talking about prepping dinner, we were quiet for the most part. Even Gid and Lex didn't harass each other. Not one finger was flipped. Now that I thought about it, I hadn't witnessed an argument, threat, or throwdown between them for weeks. Maybe my days as mediator were finally over. Whatever would I do with all the spare time that freed up?

After dinner, we loaded the dishwasher and washed pans like it was an ordinary family dinner, and we'd told Mom to take the night off while we cleaned up. Really, we used the kitchen chores as a distraction. In a few brief hours, any of us could become another tick mark on Cora's list of Teller executions. Or witnesses to our brothers' brutal murders.

The pasta sat heavy in my churning stomach.

At a quarter to midnight, we went to the backyard to wait. The moon loomed large in the sky and an ethereal glow surrounded it. Sweat trickled from the back of my neck down my spine, a combined product of humidity and fear. We took our places in the yard close to the patio and bushes where we'd hidden holy water and salt guns. Our shirts concealed the blessed ropes around our waists and bags of salt tied to our belt loops.

"No matter what happens to any of us, we fight until the end. We can't stop to help each other. Understood?" Gid asked. "Use the daggers and the other items stashed around the yard. Once Cora's restrained, we thrust the blades into her simultaneously on my count. Are we ready?"

Lex narrowed his eyes and snarled. "I was born ready."

Gid and I gave him incredulous looks. "What? Isn't that what all the greats say before they do battle—Stallone, Schwarzenegger, Willis, Reeves?"

We burst into laughter. I'd lost count of the number of times over the years I'd wanted to punch Lex's face for some of his comments. But now? His humor relieved just a smidge of the stress of this deadly situation we were in. I laughed so hard tears streamed down my face, and I wiped them away with my sleeve. Once I regained composure, I pulled my phone from my pocket and checked the time. Five minutes to go.

Gid withdrew his dagger from the sheath on his belt, the ruby at the tip of the hilt glittering in the moonlight. "Get in position."

Lex and I unsheathed our own daggers, his sapphire and mine amethyst. The cold hilt of the blade sang against my skin. We stood in a triangle, each of us facing outward in a different direction. Exactly how or where Cora would appear, we didn't know. Every muscle in my body was rigid as we waited. I inhaled deeply then exhaled slowly to calm my racing heart. It didn't help. It pounded like a jackhammer in my chest.

I felt the change in the air again, like the night Cora had appeared to us on the patio. Staticky and heavy. It raised the hair on my arms.

"She's coming," Lex said. He must have felt it, too.

The night was still, but the surrounding trees swayed as the wind picked up. My hair blew wildly about my head, and I pushed up my glasses. Lex had pulled his longer cobalt blue locks into a high ponytail in honor of Harper. A shrill cry echoed in the night air and pierced my ears. My instinct was to cover them, but I needed my hands free and ready.

It seemed Cora wanted to make a dramatic entrance.

"Over here," Gid called, and we pivoted in his direction.

Cora manifested in front of him about ten feet away. This was the moment we'd waited for. When she materialized and understood there was nobody for Iona to possess.

Gid shifted his dagger to his left hand, then whipped out a salt handgun tucked into the waistband of his jeans at his back with his right. He aimed and shot at Cora. She quickly sidestepped the pellet as it flew by her.

While the gun had distracted her, Lex pulled the rope from around his waist. He rushed toward her left side, rope looped and ready. Cora caught sight of him, raised her arm, and pushed in Lex's direction. He flew backward through the air and crashed into the patio table. Glass shattered from the impact.

I wanted to rush over and check him for injuries but remembered Gid's strict instructions.

Gid charged at Cora, dagger drawn, and I followed behind him, my blade clutched tightly in my hand. We didn't get within five feet of her. Gid's body lifted into the air. He sailed backward into me as if a crashing ocean wave had struck him. I grunted in pain when his elbow bashed into my rib as we landed in a heap of tangled limbs. The back of my head struck the ground hard.

Cora's form was solid like Macie, but she floated in the air above us. "Nice performance yesterday, but you didn't fool me. I knew you were too gutless to produce a body for Iona, and I'd have to take matters into my own hands."

I saw movement out of the corner of my eye. Lex rose from the patio. Blood trickled down his face from a cut above his right eyebrow. It was a miracle he didn't have glass shards protruding from his back. He bolted toward Cora, leaped, then grabbed onto her leg.

Cora's mask of hatred slipped into a surprised expression. He'd caught her off guard.

Lex wrestled her to the ground and quickly gained the upper hand by straddling her chest. I'd dropped my dagger when Gid and I collided, but hurriedly retrieved it from the ground and gripped it tightly in my hand. We scrambled to our feet and raced over to help Lex. We only had a moment. Gid skidded to a stop and dropped to the grass beside Cora and Lex. I sank to my knees on the other side.

"Now!" Gid called out.

Three daggers sliced through the air and plunged into—nothing but hard ground. The force of it sent shock waves up my arm into my shoulder.

Cora was no longer pinned beneath Lex. She'd disappeared. Crushing disappointment weighed heavily on my shoulders. I should have known killing her wouldn't be that easy. If it was, I'd have a large extended family instead of rows upon rows of graves in the cemetery.

Her shrill cackle ricocheted off the walls of my mind. The effect was dizzying. We yanked our daggers from the ground, then quickly stood and took defensive positions as we frantically searched the yard for Cora's location.

"Well, that was fun. I've fought multitudes of Tellers before you, and I must say the level of intelligence seems to decrease with every generation. There's nothing you can do that I haven't already faced and won."

Something Cora said earlier bothered me. She knew we'd been lying, so she'd taken matters into her own hands. I didn't know what that meant exactly, but the sound of it didn't sit right in my gut.

Gid slowly turned in a circle as he spoke, his gaze darting around the yard. "Admit it. We caught you off guard. You're scared, and that's why you ran. Come out and face us."

We stayed close to each other not only for protection, but because if another opportunity to stab her presented itself, time would be wasted if much distance separated us. Every second counted.

Something moved on my left. My brothers were in my sight, so it had to be Cora. I grabbed a handful of salt from the pouch around my waist, spun around, and hurled it in that direction.

Cora shrieked as the salt pelted her body. She continued to swoop over my head but crashed to the ground in front of the hydrangea bushes at the side of the patio. Exactly where we'd hidden a salt rifle.

"Let's go!" Gid shouted.

We sprinted across the yard.

"Lex, grab the rifle. Beck, get your rope ready. We have to wrap it around Cora to restrain her."

Lex dove into the bushes while Gid lifted his hand, dagger at the ready. I pulled the rope from my waist, ready to wrap it around Cora after Lex blasted her with the salt.

While Lex raised the gun to his shoulder and took aim, Cora rolled onto her back. Weakened from the salt, she resorted to physical violence, kicking the gun from Lex's hand then shoving Lex into the side of the house. His head cracked against the brick, and his eyes rolled back into his head. A streak of blood trailed down the wall behind him as he slid to the ground.

I raised the blessed rope, ready to toss it around her. She flinched backward as the end of it swiped against her leg. Nothing happened. When a blessed rope touched a spirit, it should weaken them, even burn. This one caused no reaction. A victorious grin spread across her face.

Gid growled as he rushed toward Cora.

Before he reached us, she ripped the rope from my hands then looped it around my neck.

I immediately threw a hand up and tried to position it between my throat and the rope, but she was too fast. I gulped in a desperate breath, knowing it could be my last.

"Stop!" Gid yelled. He stood a few feet away from us, his jaw set tight and eyes blazing. His gaze shot toward Lex then back at us.

I couldn't turn to look but didn't hear any movement. A spark of fear ignited in my belly. Lex could be severely injured. Or worse.

"You shouldn't be able to touch that rope."

"Sometimes a rope is just a rope."

I pictured the hooks that held the coils of ropes in the hidden room. Some had been stored on one side of the room with the holy water. Others hung on the opposite wall. I'd stupidly assumed all of them were blessed. Now we were paying for my mistake. I hoped Gid and Lex had taken theirs from the correct side.

"What did you think would happen here tonight?" Cora asked. "You honestly thought the three of you could kill me?" She cackled in amusement as she tightened the rope.

I struggled to draw breath into my lungs.

Anger hardened Gid's features. "You need us. Only my brothers and I can bring Iona back. Only a Teller sibling can wield the daggers."

"You forget there's another Teller sibling. One of you is expendable," Cora said as she jerked the rope, and me, toward her. I thought of Lex lying in the bushes, possibly already dead. My fate would be the same if I didn't get oxygen soon.

A snarl ripped from Gid's throat. "No! You'll never touch Harp. You have us or nothing. I'll destroy the daggers, and your daughter will be lost to you forever."

Cora squeezed the rope even tighter. Spots danced in my vision, and I knew I'd lose consciousness soon. Something dripped down my neck and into my shirt. It could only be blood or sweat. But I'd suffer through this a thousand times if it meant Harp was protected.

"You're not in control!" Cora screeched. "You *will* perform the ritual to reunite me with Iona tonight. This boy is minutes from death." She jerked the rope once more, and I fell to my knees, unable to stand any longer. Blackness creeped into the sides of my vision. "If he dies, Harper *will* take his place."

"That's impossible," Gid protested. "We don't have a body for her to inhabit." He looked at me, terror contorting his face. "Please let Beck go, I'm begging you."

"I already told you I've taken matters into my own hands. Someone will die tonight, and my daughter will live. If you do anything to harm those daggers, I'll kill the three of you, your parents, and your precious sister." Cora released the rope, and I toppled over onto my side. "Get your brothers and meet me at the cemetery."

I heard a whoosh of air when Cora departed, and then Gid was beside me. He flipped me onto my back and loosened the rope. I gulped in glorious oxygen and felt it fill my deprived lungs.

"Beck, can you hear me?"

I nodded, coughing and wheezing.

"Go check on Lex." My voice was coarse and gruff from the lack of oxygen.

Gid rose and sprinted to the bushes.

I lifted the rope over my head, rolled to my side, and slowly pushed myself up to a sitting position. My neck burned and was tender to the touch, but that was the least of my worries. There was still no movement from where Lex had fallen.

Gid shoved hydrangea leaves to the side as he made his way toward Lex. He disappeared when he kneeled behind the bushes. My heart was in my throat as I waited. Was my brother alive? I refused to consider the alternative.

The bushes rustled, and Gid stood, Lex's arm draped around his shoulder as he led him over to where I sat.

Patches of dried blood crusted along the side of Lex's face from his collision with the patio furniture. He held a hand to the back of his head. When he checked his hand, it was covered in blood. "Did we win?"

That was Lex, always asking stupid questions. He was fine.

I slowly got to my feet, my movements sluggish.

Lex stared at the blood covering his hand as he and Gid stopped in front of me. "Am I dying?"

"Head wounds bleed the worst." I prodded the back of his head. "Your brain's still inside your skull. You'll live."

"Get yourselves together," Gid said. "Cora commanded us to meet her at the cemetery, and we don't have much time."

"What she said about taking things into her own hands makes me nervous," I said. "I'm afraid to find out what that means. You don't think she—"

"Took someone?" Gid interrupted. "That's exactly what I think."

Lex rubbed the back of his head and winced. "At least we got Mom, Dad, and Harp out of here this morning. It can't be them."

Terror uncoiled from within me, and a paralyzing coldness slithered through my veins at the thought of Cora getting her hands on our parents and sister. That was impossible, right? They were out of her reach. For the moment, anyway. So, who could it be? A sense of urgency creeped over me. "We need to go now."

"Can you both walk?" Gid asked.

"Walk?" Lex asked. "I feel like we need to run. To quote Ted 'Theodore' Logan, strange things are afoot at the Circle K."

I sympathized with whomever Cora had taken. But did it make me a bad person to be happy it wasn't someone in my family?

CHAPTER TWENTY-TWO

Gid, Lex, and I raced along the wooded trail leading to the Teller family cemetery. I remembered the day Harp wandered away from me, and I'd found her there. Back when the excitement of moving into this house was still fresh and overwhelming. That was before we knew about the curse and the spirits who wandered our house and grounds. Before Cora.

Now our family was separated, two of us were injured, and my brothers and I rushed blindly toward an unknown situation. All we knew was that lives were threatened and could be lost.

The gates of the cemetery gaped open as if welcoming us inside. We slowed our pace and stopped at the entrance, unsure of what waited behind the walls. I'd never noticed lights when I'd been here before, but an ethereal glow shone beyond the gates, brightening the night. Silence cloaked the woods around us. No hoot of an owl or chitter of crickets pierced the quiet. Even the nocturnal animals knew this place was dangerous.

"Check your daggers," Gid said quietly.

I checked my sheath and felt the cold steel of the dagger hilt. Lex nodded as he patted the side of his hip where his sheath attached to his belt.

Gid nodded. "We cover each other's backs, and we fight till the end. Cora can't win."

"I know you're out there," Cora called. "Come in. We're waiting for you."

The three of us crossed the threshold into the cemetery, and I squinted as my eyes adjusted to the brighter light. The gates creaked and slammed shut behind us. Even though there were no physical locks on the gates, I didn't need to check them to know we were locked in. I continued moving forward.

Our number of weapons had dwindled. We had our daggers and the salt in the pouches tied to our belts and in our pockets, but most of the salt guns remained in the backyard. Gid still had the handgun tucked into the waistband of his jeans, but it hadn't helped much the first time he'd used it. And he still had his rope, but we couldn't be sure if it was blessed or useless like mine. Our initial plan was dead in the water.

Cora stood beneath the towering, gnarled tree in the middle of the graveyard where I'd found Harp that day. My brothers and I stayed close to each other as we walked through the symmetrical rows of graves. I had an idea why Cora had chosen this place. The graves of our relatives were a reminder of what could happen to us if we didn't play her game and abide by her rules. What the punishment would be if we broke them. I wouldn't be surprised if three new graves were already dug, just waiting for our bodies to fill them.

We stopped about fifteen feet away from her, wanting to keep some distance between us. "Come closer. You're missing the best part." Cora's eyes gleamed in anticipation like a child who couldn't wait to share a secret.

Lex and I didn't move. Neither did Gid. He said, "We're good right where we are."

Cora grinned. "Have it your way. But I bet you'll move closer when I show you the surprise." She stepped to the side, and my world turned upside down. I grabbed onto Lex's shoulder to stop me from dropping to my knees.

Aiden, Willow, and Everline kneeled on the ground, bound and gagged, their eyes wide with terror as they stared back at us.

"No!" Gid yelled. "No!" He rushed toward them, and I was right on his heels. Until we slammed into an invisible barrier that prevented us from getting any closer. Gid and I moved in opposite directions, feeling for a way in. There wasn't one.

"I was right," Cora said gleefully. "You moved closer."

"Let them go," Gid said, his voice low and threatening. "They're not Tellers, and they have nothing to do with this."

"It's your fault they're here," Cora replied. "I'd never have known about Aiden or Willow if you hadn't brought them to this house. If not for that, they'd probably be home safe and sound in their own beds right now, completely unaware of the danger they're in just by being around you."

I remembered the night I'd come home from the hospital after Dad's injury to find Aiden and Gid in the lounge chair on the patio. I'd been overwhelmed with a sense that a mistake had been made. I'd again worried when Willow visited the next morning after Everline had told me to keep her away from the house.

"I compelled them to come here. They didn't know why, only that they needed to get here to see you. And this one," Cora gestured toward Everline, "followed Willow. Everline is no stranger to this house. She's visited several times, but always seemed to sense something wasn't quite right." Cora turned to look at Everline. "Your instincts were correct."

Everline glared back at her, hatred burning in her eyes.

I'd gone to the bookstore that afternoon after Willow stopped by my house. I knew she'd eventually tell Everline she'd been there, but I thought it would be better if she heard it from me first. She hadn't been pleased, but Everline knew her granddaughter was concerned about me, and I'd had nothing to do with bringing her into the house. Both of us hoped nothing would come of it.

We'd been horribly, horribly wrong.

"What do you want?" I asked. "We'll give you anything. Just don't hurt them. Please."

"What do I want?" Cora seemed taken aback at my question. "My deal hasn't changed. One of these people will be sacrificed so my daughter can live again. I admit, having the soul of a ten-year-old girl in the body of an old woman, or a teenager—especially a boy— might be strange at first, but I'd grow accustomed to it." She sneered. "But you haven't learned the best part yet. I'll let you three choose who it is."

Willow's eyes pleaded with me as silent tears streamed down her face. I yearned to run to her and shield her from Cora, pounded on the barrier to try and break in, but Cora kept us at a distance. A distance that felt like miles. Aiden might have been a go-with-the-flow kind of guy, but the maniacal gleam in his eye as he glared at Cora made me wonder if that disguised the serial killer inside him. Gid's hands clenched and unclenched, and he muttered curses under his breath. He was just as desperate to get to Aiden as I was to Willow and Everline.

"You can't force us to choose," Gid said. "We won't do it."

Cora slowly rose into the air and looked down at us, her expression haughty and menacing. "Fine. I won't force you to do anything. But know this. If you choose, the other two live. If I choose, then I'll kill the other two. Would you rather be responsible for three deaths or one? You may have a few minutes to discuss it."

All the breath left my body, and Gid slumped beside me. This was an impossible situation. We'd already lost. No matter what happened, we'd sentence someone to die tonight. Probably all of us when it was all over. Cora would keep me and my brothers alive long enough to bring back Iona, but she had no use for us after that. The same went for whomever didn't contain Iona's spirit. Six people would die tonight.

The three of us gathered in a huddle.

"We can't let them die," Lex said.

"No one's dying," Gid said. "I'll sacrifice myself first."

"You can't," I protested. "Remember, it takes all three of us to perform the ritual, and Cora said she'd never allow Iona to possess a Teller body."

"I wasn't talking about letting her take over my body," Gid looked intently first at me, then Lex. "I mean killing myself, so Cora doesn't get what she wants, and no one else has to die."

I squeezed my eyes shut, his words too painful to process. I couldn't lose my brother. Hearing Gid's offer to give up his life so all of us could live wasn't surprising. Protecting and taking care of his family had always been at the heart of nearly everything he did. He loved us. And he loved Aiden. That much was obvious. Willow and Everline were practically strangers to him, but he still didn't want anyone outside the family to fall victim to the curse. It was a completely selfless offer.

But it wouldn't work.

"Even if you did that, Cora still wins. She'd make Harp take your place. We know Cora can get to her and Mom and Dad. And after Cora gets what she wants, we all die."

Gid ran his hands through his hair in frustration. "Then what can we do? Choosing one of them isn't an option. None of us can sacrifice ourselves. If we try to destroy the daggers, we all die. Our plan to take Cora out first was a disaster. We still have one rope that may or may not be blessed. She's too strong for us to overpower. What's left?"

"Begging and pleading," Lex said.

"We've done that, too," I reminded him.

The defeated expressions on their faces matched my own. We'd run out of options. Cora had backed us into a corner, and there was only one way out. Giving someone else a death sentence.

Gid squeezed his eyes tightly shut, his hands fisted at his side. When he opened them, his decision was made. "We have to choose."

"Your time is running out," Cora said. "I need an answer."

My gaze turned to the three hostages. Although bound, gagged, and completely at Cora's mercy, Aiden stayed upright on his knees, defiant to the end. Willow leaned her head over on Everline's shoulder. Everline's head tilted into hers as she offered what little comfort she could. Her eyes met mine, her silent plea communicated with only a look. I knew exactly what she was asking. That didn't make it any less difficult. She may be my employer and I hadn't known her for long, but I loved Everline. She was a kind and generous woman who felt like family.

"It has to be Everline," I said. "It's what she wants. She'd do anything to protect Willow, and she'd never want Aiden to die for her."

"I don't want to do this," Lex said. "How do we live with ourselves after this is over? Suppose the ritual works. What if Iona picks up where she left off, and she and Cora go on a mother/daughter nationwide killing spree? What happens then?"

Gid placed his hand on Lex's shoulder. "We'll deal with that if it happens. Right now, we need to save as many lives as we can."

We reluctantly turned to face Cora.

"It's Everline," I said, regret thick in my voice. My eyes met hers, and I hoped she saw the apology in mine. Whether or not she could, Everline looked relieved. Grateful we didn't choose Willow or Aiden. Willow screamed, then sobbed over the gag in her mouth. I wanted so badly to wrap my arms around her and hoped she understood the reason for our decision. Maybe in time she would, though I didn't see how. By condemning her grandmother, I'd ended our relationship. And that was a best-case scenario.

Still hovering above the hostages, Cora lowered herself to the ground and moved in front of Everline and her granddaughter. She gazed down at them, a depraved smile splitting her lips. "Such a beautiful, loving relationship. Like the one I had with my daughter. I almost hate to pull you from each other. Almost." She grabbed Willow's shoulder and yanked her to her feet. Everline screamed and tried to stand but fell to her side. I gaped at Willow in horror. "This is the body Iona will take over."

"No!" I screamed, lunging forward. Gid grabbed my upper arm and pulled me back before I slammed into the barrier. "You said it was our choice, and we chose Everline!"

"No. Everline chose Everline. As with everything else you endeavor to do, you were too weak to do this. Besides, it would be too strange for my daughter to be older than me. This girl is the obvious choice."

Willow looked down at her grandmother, her shoulders heaving with silent sobs. Cora grabbed her chin and forced Willow to look into her maniacal eyes. "We'll have many happy years together. The life my daughter and I should have had long ago."

I gripped the sides of my head, and my body trembled from head to toe. Rage threatened to rip me into pieces if I didn't let it out. I was the logical brother, the one who rationalized and negotiated. Not the one who exploded in rage or joked my way out of situations. But right now, logic, rationale, and negotiation were useless tactics. Right now, violence and anger won.

I roared as I rammed my shoulder against the barrier over and over, desperate to break through and get to Willow.

Lex wrapped his arms around my waist and pulled me away from it.

Gid grabbed my shoulders, his face only inches from mine.

"You've got to stop, Beck. You'll only hurt yourself and then you're no good to anyone. Breathe. We won't let this happen. I don't know how, but we'll find a way. You need to stay with us. Remember what Macie said about the number three. Balance, completeness, and harmony. If three forces come together, they can generate a greater impact or achieve a desired outcome. We've got this, but only if you're with us."

I stared back at him intently, my jaw clenched and my breaths hard and fast. I nodded. Lex's grip loosened around my waist. My hand immediately flew to my dagger. I unsheathed it, raised it over my head, and thrust it into the invisible barrier again and again. I didn't know if it would work, but we were out of options. Sweat poured down my face from the exertion. Something gave, and my blade sank in further. "It's working!" I yelled.

Gid and Lex hurriedly withdrew their own daggers and mimicked my actions.

Chaos reigned behind the barrier. Willow tried to shake off Cora and stay with Everline. Although his hands were bound, Aiden threw himself between Cora and Willow. Cora roared with anger and frustration as she was forced to split her attention between them and the three of us as we chipped away at the wall that separated us. Part of me leaped with joy over the fact that this situation wasn't going as she'd expected.

I drew back my arm and stabbed at the wall with all my force. Instead of the expected resistance, I fell forward.

We were through.

I sprinted through the rows of graves and tombstones toward Willow, Aiden, and Everline, Gid and Lex on my heels. Cora flitted through the air between us. She still had the power to hurt us without using her hands. I felt a ripple in the air behind me.

Gid grunted, lowering his voice. "Keep going!"

Something tangled around my legs, and I plummeted to the ground, slamming my shoulder into a headstone. When I reached to unravel whatever it was, nothing was there. I immediately climbed to my feet as Lex dashed past me. He got to the hostages first. I was right behind him.

Gid's dagger slashed through the air at Cora as he distracted her from what we were doing. It wouldn't work for long.

"Untie them. Hurry." I didn't need to say anything. Lex had already ripped the gag from Aiden's mouth and was sawing on the rope binding his hands.

I pulled off Willow's and Everline's gags. "I'm sorry. I'm so sorry."

Everline shook her head. "No apologies. You did what I wanted you to do. And it's not over yet."

"You need to get out of here. Run and don't look back." I untied Willow's hands, and she turned to release Everline while I cut through the binding around her ankles.

"What about you and your brothers?" Willow asked.

I looped my arm around Everline and helped her stand. "Don't worry about us. I just need to know you're nowhere near here." My gaze darted to Gid.

Cora pushed her arms toward him, and he rocketed backward through the air. He dropped to the ground, rolled, and came to rest against a headstone.

"Please, Willow. Go. Now."

Willow nodded through her tears and took Everline's arm. "Thank you."

"Don't you go dying on me, Beck Teller," Everline said.

"I'll do my best, boss. Now run." I watched as they rushed toward the gates and prayed they weren't still locked. I spun back to Lex and Aiden, but they weren't there. They'd run over to Gid. Lex stood in front of him, dagger out, facing Cora alone. Aiden used that distraction to help Gid to his feet. I sprinted in their direction. Whatever happened, the three of us needed to stay together.

"What are you still doing here? Run!" Gid yelled at Aiden.

Aiden shook his head. "I'm not leaving. I'm staying with you."

"Need some help here," Lex called out.

Cora hovered above him as Lex continued to slash at her with his blade. I took up position on the other side of Cora. Her back was to me as she concentrated on Lex, Gid, and Aiden. I reached into my salt pouch, grabbed a handful, then flung it at her. The spray of salt hit her back, and she screeched in pain. Cora whipped in my direction, her face a mask of anger.

Gid pulled the rope from his waist. He held one end while Aiden grabbed the other. They wanted to wrap it around Cora while Lex and I distracted her.

After the salt hit her, Cora dropped closer to the ground. "Grab her leg!" I called to Lex, but he'd already figured out the plan. Lex sheathed his dagger then leaped into the air. Once his hands gripped Cora's ankle, he jerked her toward the ground.

She howled with rage and kicked Lex in the face. His head fell backward, and blood gushed from his nose, but he held tight.

I grabbed her other ankle.

She struggled and hissed at us.

"Release me!"

"Not a chance, demon spawn," Lex snapped through gritted teeth.

Gid and Aiden moved in, and I hoped with everything inside me this rope was blessed. The second it touched her skin, I had my answer. Cora screeched and contorted in pain. They wrapped it around her waist then pulled her to the ground. Lex and I immediately pinned her arms to her sides. She continued to spit curses at us, but I focused on restraining her as Gid and Aiden tied her down.

We finally had the upper hand. This nightmare was almost over.

"Draw your daggers," Gid said.

Lex and I unsheathed our blades. The jeweled hilts glittered in the moonlight. Gid's ruby for energy and power. Lex's sapphire for clarity, peace, and wisdom. My amethyst that banished and warded off spirits.

Cora continued to writhe beneath us, fighting to the end.

We raised our blades.

"On my count," Gid said. "One, two, thr—"

"They're here! They're here!" A voice called. A voice I knew very well. But that was impossible. We'd sent them away this morning. They were supposed to be safe in a motel miles away from here. "Get away from my brothers!" Harper screamed.

The four of us whipped our heads in her direction, and that split second of us letting down our guard was all Cora needed. She released a burst of energy that hit us square in the chests. Gid, Lex, Aiden, and I exploded into the air as if a grenade had gone off.

I crashed to the ground. A stab of pain shot through my shoulder.

Cora ripped the blessed rope from her body, palm steaming and dead flesh burning. She flung it to the ground then soared into the air, cackling.

Harper ran through the rows of graves in our direction, her auburn curls trailing behind her in a wave. Mom and Dad were on her heels. Behind them, I saw Willow and Everline exit through the gate. At least there were two fewer people to worry about. But life just delivered us a dumpster full of more problems. Our parents and Harper were in danger.

I climbed slowly to my feet, leaning on a headstone for support, and made my way over to them. "Why are you here?"

The guys were right on my heels. A fresh cut over Lex's left eye matched the one on his right. Aiden limped along as he favored one leg. Blood dripped from Gid's split lip. He winced as he scooped up Harper. Lex and I stood guard, our backs turned toward them.

"We came to save you," Harp said, her voice scratchy.

My heart sank. We'd been a second away from saving ourselves when she arrived.

Our parents stood in paralyzed horror, staring at Cora floating above us. She circled our group like a vulture waiting for its prey to die. A dark grin contorted her ugly features, as if our family reunion thrilled her. And why wouldn't it? She had all of us in one place at her mercy. Surely another attack was imminent.

"Mom!" Gid yelled.

She brought her attention to him, her eyes wild with fear. "Harp woke up screaming, inconsolable. She insisted we needed to get back. Bad things were happening."

"We talked about this. We all decided the best way to protect her was to stay away. She's in danger." Gid tried to pass Harper to Mom.

"Don't blame your mother," Dad said. "You didn't hear Harp's screams. We had no choice."

Inconsolable screaming explained why her voice sounded like she'd smoked a pack of cigarettes.

Harp punched Gid's shoulder and squirmed against him. "I'm not leaving! I can bring the light and help you!"

"Take her." Gid again attempted to push her into Mom's arms as Harp fought against them.

Then my world exploded.

Cora swooped toward us, moving far too quickly. Lex and I fumbled in our bags and hurled salt at her, but she easily dodged it.

"Gid!" I screamed.

He spun toward us as he shoved Harper and Mom behind him, but it was too late. Cora dove, plucked Harper from Mom's arms, then flew toward the mangled tree. Screams of terror erupted from our parents as they chased after Cora.

"No! Not her!" Gid roared. "Harp, hang on!"

"Let me go!" Harp yelled. "You said you were my friend!"

Cora landed softly on the ground in front of the tree. At least she hadn't harmed Harper. Yet, anyway. My sister faced us as Cora's dead hands gripped her shoulders, holding her in place.

Harp wasn't making it easy. She struggled to get free and kicked at Cora. We all dashed toward them, dodging tombstones, and hopping over graves.

Fear for my sister ran cold through my veins. But fury ran alongside it. I was so angry at my parents for bringing her back. Cora getting her hands on Harper was the worst possible scenario. The exact thing we'd tried to prevent.

"Stay back!" Cora's attention darted down at Harper then back to us, her message clear. Harp would pay the consequences if we intervened. "No more stunts. It's time to begin the ritual. Harper is my choice, and Iona will possess her body. I'll finally have my little girl back."

Mom screamed.

"You said you'd never allow your daughter to inhabit a Teller's body," I said, desperate to change Cora's mind and make her see Harper wasn't an option.

"Harper is young, a few years younger than Iona when she died. She's not tainted like the rest of you Tellers." Cora ran her hand over Harp's hair. "Maybe this is the way it should have been all along. Klaus, Karl, and Hans took my daughter. Now I'll take Joshua's."

My stomach knotted in desperation and fear. This couldn't be happening. Surely it was a wicked nightmare. The worst of my life.

"Don't take her," Gid pleaded. "We'll do anything. Please. Not Harper."

Mom sobbed quietly against Dad's shoulder. His face was drained of color, even paler than the evening of his injury, if that was possible.

I turned my attention to Harper. She stood in front of Cora, but she'd stopped fighting. Her eyes squinched closed as if she was concentrating hard on something.

The light. I remembered what she'd told me. She closed her eyes, concentrated, and brought the light. She'd said the light would help us. I didn't know how or what her plan was, but we needed to give her time to do it.

We wouldn't have much.

"It's time," Cora said. "Come forward with your daggers. Iona is waiting."

Mom fell to her knees, her hands clasped together in front of her. "I'm begging you, as one mother to another, please don't do this. You know the devastating pain of losing a child. You've felt it for over a century. Look at everything you've done to be with your daughter again."

Cora tilted her head back slightly, chin in the air, as if it was beneath her to even acknowledge Mom. "Yes, I know the pain of losing a child. It's no longer my burden to bear. It's time another

Teller lives with such pain." She looked back at Gid. "The daggers. Now."

A howl of sorrow escaped from Mom as Dad helped her to her feet. The two of them pulled each of us in for a hug. Aiden reached for Gid's hand and squeezed it, then the three of us trudged forward to where Cora held Harper. Cora fully expected us to kill our sister so her daughter could live. We'd plunge the daggers into our own chests before we'd let anyone touch Harp. And that's exactly what my brothers and I had planned to do as a last resort. We were down to the wire. No time was left.

We stopped in front of Cora. Harp's eyes were still tightly closed. Her tiny right hand slowly rose above her head. The air shifted around us and prickled the back of my neck.

Cora lifted her gaze and focused on something behind us, her features twisted in confusion. The surrounding light grew brighter.

"What's happening?" Cora asked.

My brothers and I turned in the direction of Cora's gaze. A bright open doorway stood among the tombstones, brilliant golden light streaming from inside it. I looked back to Harper. Her eyes were open, and she smiled widely. "I told you I could bring the light."

"Look at all of them," Lex whispered.

Spirits arrived at the cemetery from every direction—through the gates and walls, from the trees and graves, even from thin air. All Tellers Cora had killed. They were drawn to the doorway like moths to a flame after being trapped here for so long.

It was enough to give Cora pause.

My parents and Aiden looked around in confusion, sensing something big was happening based on our words and expressions. I wasn't sure why they were able to see Cora but not the spirits. We'd have to explain their appearance and the doorways later.

Cora scrutinized Harper intently. "It was you? You're the one who opened the door and let Teller spirits cross over?"

"Yep," Harper said, very pleased with herself. Then she glared darkly at Cora. "You're not a nice person for hurting them and making them stay here. They're my family, and I helped them."

Flames of rage lit Cora's eyes, and her body shook with anger. I readied myself to jump between Cora and Harp if she lashed out at my sister. Harp's actions had overridden part of Cora's curse. After all these years, her plans were foiled by a six-year-old girl.

"What are they doing?" Gid asked.

The Teller spirits gathered around the door but weren't going through. They remained on this side as if waiting for something. Judging by the way they glared with hatred at Cora, maybe it was revenge. She'd taken so much from all of them.

"Guess what else I can do?" Harp asked. Her voice didn't quaver in the least.

I was in awe of her bravery. And so very proud.

Once again, Harper squeezed her eyes shut and raised her hand. We watched as another door appeared beside the other. But this one wasn't golden. It was dark and worn with age. A heaviness settled in my chest when I looked at it, and the world suddenly seemed desolate. Evil lived beyond its threshold.

"What is that?" Cora whispered.

"The pretty door leads to the good place," Harper explained. "But not everyone gets to go there. Some people are mean, like you. They go through the other door."

The dark door slowly creaked open. Decaying vines creeped over the threshold then wrapped around the doorframe. A heavy gray mist swirled out behind them. It snaked through the tombstones and past the Teller spirits who waited in front of the golden doorway, then continued past Mom, Dad, and Aiden, who were unaware of its presence.

Cora clutched at her throat and backed away from Harper.

"It's here for you," Harp said. "You can't run from it."

The icy mist weaved around our legs as if searching for something. For Cora. Then, almost as if it smelled her, it shot forward and coiled around her waist.

"No!" Cora screamed.

We watched with a mixture of horror and delight as the mist jerked her off her feet, dragged her through the graves and past all the people she'd killed, then yanked her through the doorway. Her shrieks echoed in the night.

I sheathed my dagger, lunged toward Harper, then picked her up and held her close.

Gid and Lex moved toward us, then stopped. Gid's face contorted in confusion. Lex turned his dagger over in his palm and studied it.

"What is it?" I asked. Then I felt movement at my waist. My dagger quivered in its sheath before an invisible force tore it away.

Gid and Lex yelped in surprise as their daggers were ripped from their hands. The three blades shot into the air and hurled through the doorway behind Cora. The ground vibrated beneath us as the dark door slammed shut. Then it disappeared.

I turned my attention back to Harp and hugged her tightly. "You're safe," was all I could say over and over. Gid and Lex piled into us, and I didn't know whose arms were whose. Our parents and Aiden rushed over, reasoning the danger must be over since Cora was gone and group hugs were happening. Gid caught Aiden in his arms as he tackle-hugged him.

Harper wiggled in my arms. "Put me down. We have to say goodbye."

For a split second, my heart cracked when I thought she meant to say goodbye to us. I set her down to explain she was safe, but she wasn't looking at me. She waved at all the Teller spirits who still waited by the door.

They smiled brightly at her. So many of them. Men, women, and children of all ages. One by one, they filtered through the doorway to their final resting place and peace at long last.

Macie appeared beside us, still regal in her pearls. "Saying 'thank you' isn't enough for everything you did."

"It was Harper," I said. "She saved us all."

Macie beamed with happiness at my sister.

"Someone's waiting for you." Harp pointed toward the door.

The young girl in the white dress who'd helped me locate the daggers stood by the doorway, a doll clutched to her chest.

Emily, Macie's daughter.

Macie rushed past us to Emily and took her in her arms. They looked back at us once more, and Macie waved. Then mother and daughter stepped through the doorway. It closed gently behind them then vanished.

"Does anyone have a tissue?" Lex asked.

Count on him to ruin a wonderful moment.

CHAPTER TWENTY-THREE

A week had passed since the terrifying showdown in the cemetery. Our lives returned to normal. Or as normal as they could be after the horrors we'd experienced.

For the second time, our incredible, completely amazing little sister saved our family. Maybe if Harper hadn't demanded to come back, my brothers and I would have killed Cora with the daggers. But maybe not. We'd never know.

Harp explained the daggers followed Cora through the doorway because something bad was in them. Cora's daughter, Iona. In the end, Cora's wish was granted. She was reunited with her daughter—just not in the way she'd hoped.

Mom also got her wish. Willow and Aiden were coming for dinner tonight, along with Everline. Gid and I pleaded with her to make it casual and not a more formal occasion in the dining room where Willow and Aiden would feel like they were being interviewed. She'd agreed to keep it simple. Dad was grilling burgers in the backyard, and the table was set on the patio. Gid and I also threatened Lex about keeping his snide comments to himself. He swore he would, but I honestly didn't know if it was something he could control.

The doorbell rang. It had to be Willow and Everline, as Aiden was already here and with Gid on the patio helping Dad, who was still basically operating with one arm. I opened the door, and Willow immediately came in and hugged me. Any lingering doubts about whether she was angry with me for choosing her grandmother faded when her arms wrapped around me. Then she pulled back and gave me a quick kiss on the lips. Blood creeped up my face as Everline watched from behind her. It was still all kinds of awkward showing affection in front of her, but she didn't seem to mind.

"Hello, Beck," Everline said. "I'll skip the kiss, if you don't mind."

"Um, yeah, that's fine."

When I'd turned up at the bookstore the afternoon after the showdown, Everline embraced me tightly for the longest time. Even Mr. Darcy gave me extra head bonks as if he'd sensed the danger I'd been in. When Everline released me, she thanked me.

"Words can't express how grateful I am for what you did for Willow and me." I opened my mouth to protest, to say it was my fault. I was sick with guilt that they'd been in danger, and I could barely face her after offering her to Cora.

She held up a hand to silence me. "None of this was your fault. Willow went to your house of her own accord. No one could have predicted any of what followed. And you did the right thing in the graveyard. Now, we never have to speak of it again. Understand?"

I didn't. I had about three million more apologies in me.

Before I could offer even one, she scolded me for coming in. "After all your family has been through, you need to be home with them. Take some time to rest, Beck." Then she grinned. "I sure am glad you didn't die on me."

Yeah, she was family now. But I agreed with her. No kissing.

"I brought a bottle of wine for your parents," she said, holding it out.

I took the bottle, then entwined my fingers with Willow's and led them through the house to the backyard.

"It's strange being in this house again without Macie." She glanced into the parlor where Macie and Elizabeth had played backgammon. "But I'm glad it's full of happiness now."

The thought or mention of Macie always brought a smile to my lips. I missed her, but I was so happy she was with her daughter. Her life had been sad and lonely for far too long. I also missed Elizabeth. Doing my own laundry wasn't fun. I'd started using the coasters she'd left around the house in her honor. I think she'd be proud.

Mom and Dad greeted Everline like they'd been friends for years. I expected she wouldn't be a stranger at our house. Gid and Aiden sat on a couch, their clasped hands resting on Gid's leg. Lex spoke animatedly to them, his hands waving in the air. I'm sure it was another of his highly embellished stories, judging by Gid's skeptical expression.

Gid announced at family dinner a couple nights ago that he's considering continuing in the paranormal business. Do I really need to say it didn't sit well with Mom and Dad? He'd reached out to the Broussard family in New Orleans Macie had mentioned, and they'd offered to train him. He promised our parents to give it more thought and stay here at least one more year until Aiden graduated high school. After that, if Gid decided to go to New Orleans, Aiden was going with him.

After what we'd been through, I wanted no part of the paranormal business. A quiet life working in the bookstore, going to school, and dating Willow were my priorities for the foreseeable future, but I'd support Gid in any way I could.

Willow and I sat on a glider on the other side of the patio, away from everyone, our hands still entwined. I squeezed her fingers. "Thanks for not breaking up with me."

"You think being kidnapped by an evil spirit who planned to let her daughter possess my body would drive me away? What kind of person do you think I am?" The look she gave me flushed warmth through my whole body. "But I have to admit, I'm ready for less exciting dates now. How about the amusement park at the pier tomorrow night?"

"Sounds perfect." I leaned in to kiss her. Since Everline wasn't right in front of us, I made sure this kiss lasted longer. Until a giggle from the hydrangea bush behind us cut it short. "Come on out, Harp."

She skipped around the side of the bush carrying Rex, Loki, and Percy, then crawled up into my lap.

After Harper answered our questions about that night, she refused to talk about it anymore. We'd known she could open the golden doorway, but the dark doorway came as a shock. To Harper, it made perfect sense. "There are nice and not nice people in the world, so there have to be doorways for both." The world explained in black and white, courtesy of a six-year-old. I wished life was always that simple for her.

Harp grinned at Willow. "I'm glad you're still Beck's girlfriend. His last one was pretend."

Willow laughed. "Can you tell me more about this fake girlfriend?"

I'd known from the first day we arrived at this house our lives would be forever changed, but I could never have predicted it would turn out like this. Now we could put down roots and become part of a community. No more wondering how long we'd be in a new place or putting off making friends or dating because we didn't want to face painful goodbyes. Without the curse hanging over our heads, we could enjoy our beautiful permanent home and get on with our lives.

I looked around the patio at my friends and family, listened to their loud laughter, and grinned. We were off to a good start.

ACKNOWLEDGEMENTS

Writing a book is rarely a solo project. I'd never be able to get this novel into the world without the help of many others.

Editor Staci Troilo is the absolute best. My timeline with this novel was tight, and she performed miracles.

My son Reese brainstormed with me numerous times when I was trying to connect the dots in this story, and he offered creative advice and ideas. His ability to think outside the box was evident from a young age, and now his D&D groups and I benefit from it.

Susan, Lynne, and Bonnie (now you're a character in a book!) are always patient listeners and the occasional captive audience when I drone on about story ideas. Susan also rescued this novel when Word flashed the dreaded corrupt file message, and my vision darkened in panic. Infinite thanks for that!

My physician brother-in-law Chris answered my medical questions. Any incorrect information is his fault. Just kidding! It's totally mine.

Fallon, Jolene, and Val gave feedback during the early stages of this book during summer writing camp. You guys were awesome virtual cabin mates!

Deanna read early and later drafts and always offers honest, valuable critiques. She also caught typos four other readers missed proving once again that no matter the number of eyes on a project, it's rarely error free.

Thanks to fellow horror fan Macie Wheeler for letting me borrow your name. The pearls were Susan's idea.

To the bloggers and readers who are passionate about books, tell anyone willing (or unwilling) to listen about them, and write book reviews—you're my people.

Reagan and the team at Black Rose Writing are always incredibly supportive and work tirelessly for their authors.

Last, but certainly not least, thanks to my family and friends for their support. If total strangers accosted you on the street and told you about my books, you've met some of them.

ABOUT THE AUTHOR

Teri Polen is the author of young adult horror, science fiction, and fantasy novels. *Sarah*, her debut novel, was a horror finalist in the 2017 Next Generation Indie Book Awards. ReadFREE.ly named *Subject A36* one of the 50 Best Indie Books of 2020. An avid reader, movie watcher, and chocolate lover, Teri lives in Bowling Green, KY with her husband and Feline Overlord, Bond. Visit her at TeriPolen.com or on Instagram @Tpolen6

OTHER TITLES BY TERI POLEN

NOTE FROM TERI POLEN

Word-of-mouth is crucial for any author to succeed. If you enjoyed *The Power of Three*, please leave a review online—anywhere you are able. Even if it's just a sentence or two. It would make all the difference and would be very much appreciated.

Thanks!

Teri Polen

We hope you enjoyed reading this title from:

www.blackrosewriting.com

Subscribe to our mailing list – *The Rosevine* – and receive **FREE** books, daily
deals, and stay current with news about upcoming
releases and our hottest authors.
Scan the QR code below to sign up.

Already a subscriber? Please accept a sincere thank you for being a fan of
Black Rose Writing authors.

View other Black Rose Writing titles at
www.blackrosewriting.com/books and use promo code
PRINT to receive a **20% discount** when purchasing.